IRENE HARRINGTON

THE
· SUITCASE ·

DEDICATION

This book is dedicated to Joanna and Allison Evans.

Thank you for allowing me to write this beautiful story about your uncle, James H. Evans, and your family. When someone asked if he had a family, he would proudly say, "Yes! I have two nieces. They are very smart, also." Never forget the love that was shared in your family. He loved you girls so much. It didn't start with your Uncle James and his brothers, but it started many years ago. You girls are the product of that beginning.

Each friend represents a world in us—a world not born until they arrive—and it is only by this meeting that a new world is born. The first phone call, the first meeting, I never thought our worlds would collide to form the relationship we now have with each other. When your uncle's health failed him, another world was arriving. And now, a new world is born.

We must keep the faith. Learn from what we have seen and heard. Remember the best of these times and embrace the sorrow of losing a loved one and a friend. In the midst of all of life's disappointments, the truths and untruths, tears and smiles, there's a soft sweet spirit that is near us whispering, "You girls did a great job and I love you for it."

~ Irene Harrington

INTRODUCTION

Memories of our lives, of our works, and our deeds will continue in others long after we are gone.

This quote best describes the works, deeds, and the love that James Evans extended to all he touched throughout his life.

The adult life of educator and philanthropist James Evans began in Wadesboro, North Carolina, in 1960 at a small school in the Lilesville community. He was a Christian man who loved the Lord and tried to treat his fellow man as brothers and children of God. James didn't allow obstacles to get in his way when it came to caring for his mother, his students, and his neighbors. He proudly served his country and later pursued his education at the school that his grandfather helped build. James lived alone but made many dear friends during his stay in Anson County.

A terrible disease captured the nation and thousands died. James was one in that number. The whole county was devastated by the news. It was his time, and he was aware of what his Lord and Savior was doing. He was prepared to leave all his memories for others to learn from.

He fulfilled the dream of his parents. They knew that the man they raised would be prosperous and be a good example to all.

As a professional black man in rural Anson County, North Carolina, he made a mark in the community by giving of his time, his friendship and his resources to those who needed them.

This is the unforgettable story of an unforgettable man.

TABLE OF CONTENTS

Dedication..3

Introduction..4

Chapter 1..7

Chapter 2..17

Chapter 3..22

Chapter 4..30

Chapter 5..34

Chapter 6..38

Chapter 7..41

Chapter 8..44

Chapter 9..49

Chapter 10..54

Chapter 11..59

Chapter 12..66

Chapter 13..75

Chapter 14..81

Chapter 15..87

Chapter 16..92

Chapter 17..99

Chapter 18..107

Chapter 19..113

Chapter 20..117

Chapter 21..120

Chapter 22..126

Chapter 23..130

Chapter 24..134

Chapter 25..146

Chapter 26..153

Chapter 27..155

Evans Family Photos...157

MR. JAMES EVANS

CHAPTER 1

•••

It was bone-chillingly cold on that October morning in 1895, as Sarah boarded the train for her destination. She was all alone. Tears flowed down her cheeks as she thought about her mother and the town she loved so dearly. Having to leave all her friends and the people she knew for many years was heartbreaking. During the spring of that year, there was a terrible outbreak of an unknown disease that hit the community. Hundreds, maybe thousands of people died in that small town of Virginia, including her mother.

Sarah worked hard in the tobacco fields for months to earn her train fare. There was little time to buy warm clothing from the country store, so she made room in her small bag for what she had.

The train was crowded with many passengers, including soldiers leaving from Germany. As she walked through the packed aisle, she spotted an empty space large enough for a person her size. There was a young man staring at her. "Sir," she asked, "Is anyone sitting next to you?" Without saying a word, the man got up and offered her the seat. Sarah thanked him and sat down. He stood there for a moment and paused. Before he sat down, he took a folded newspaper from his coat pocket and began reading. He soon looked Sarah's way and asked, "Are you from this area?" Sarah grabbed her bag and held it close to her side. "Yes," she said, as she looked down at the floor.

"I'm trying to get back to my home. I've been all over the world. I joined the war when I was only 17 years old. I want to see my family and friends now. My daddy needs someone to help on the farm. I never did write to them, because I knew I would be home before they get the letter," he said, as he waited on Sarah for a reply. She didn't know what to say. Her mother always told her not to talk to strangers, but something was different about this man. The man continued to turn the pages of the newspaper. "Would you like a snack or something to drink?" he asked. Sarah didn't want to be rude, so she decided to answer since he was nice enough to give her a seat. "No, Sir. I have my own thank you." He opened his Army bag and took out a bar of candy and his canteen of water. "I ate so many of these bars when I was overseas, now I'm tired of eating this stuff! They said it was good for us. All type of nutrients and vitamins in them, they said, but who knows! They tell us anything, as long as we're fighting their stupid war." The man took off his hat and coat. He pushed the back of his seat down and told Sarah he was going to take a nap. She didn't say a word. The view outside was beautiful and she didn't want to miss seeing the countryside.

An hour had passed. Sarah needed to get up and stretch her legs. "Sir, sir," she said, but he did not answer. She touched him lightly on his shoulder. The man opened his eyes, and said calmly, "Honey, what do you need?" Sarah's heart skipped a beat. No one had never called her "Honey." "I need to stand for a little bit and stretch my legs," she said. He stood and let her out. "Are you sure you're okay? I'll stay here and watch your bags if you want to walk around a bit." Sarah didn't know what to think. She agreed and then thanked the man. An emptiness inside of her felt as if God himself was filling it up. She remembered her mother telling her that God was going to send the right man for her someday.

As she walked through the train, there was a feeling of being needed by someone, and that felt good. She walked with pride and security. *"Oh God, please! I have never been in love, and don't know how it feels. If this man is who you want me to have in my life, please show it to me. And if it's not, don't let me make a fool of myself,"* she prayed.

As she neared her seat, the man stood to let her in. As he took his seat, he put the newspaper in his coat pocket, and said, "By the way, I didn't tell you my name. William Clingman standing before you, my dear!" He offered Sarah his hand. She shook it and said, "Glad to meet you, Mr. Clingman." Sarah was beyond herself. She felt comfortable having a nice, young, handsome man—and mannerly too—to sit by her side. "You can call me William. Now, what might be your name?" he asked. "Sarah is my name. I'm sorry for not being friendlier, but where I'm from, young ladies don't talk to strangers. You know Sir, I mean, William, you are the first man I have met since my school days at home. There weren't a lot of young men in my neighborhood. I'm glad to meet you," she said with a smile. William smiled at her and asked if she wanted to read his newspaper.

"There's so much going on in the world these days, I hate to look at the paper! But we got to keep up with what's going on in our country. I don't want to go back to war. I want to settle down, buy some land, get married and have me a family. What about you, Sarah?" he asked. Sarah looked down at her hands, folded her arms and said, "I would love to have a family someday. I always felt like I would make a good mother and wife. My momma taught me so much about being the best at anything I wanted to be. She taught me how to sew, cook, clean a house, and work outside the home. She also told me that a man wants a woman who can do most of anything. I've been working since I was 10 years old. I worked in the tobacco fields after my father died. I had to learn to cook and clean the house at an early age. I don't regret the way she raised me. She knew someday she would leave me, and I had to do for myself. 'You can tell if a man is a good man by the way he treats woman,' she would say. 'Look at his shoes to see if he is clean. Look at his hands to see if he will work. And most of all, if he is an honest man, most likely he loves his God.' That's what I was taught in my home. I don't think the way I was raised will ever leave me. You can only be what your parents put in you!" she said, as William listened and took it all in.

"Your momma taught you well. I like everything I have heard. My parents are dead, too. My momma died when I was 16 years old. My daddy died on the plantation where we lived. Now, you talk about a man! He was a man! He was well-educated by one of the pastors on the plantation. He taught other people to read and write. It came natural to him. That old pastor would show my daddy a book and explain the words and how the letters came together, and he could read it! He could add his money and knew how much change you owed him. He could have been a teacher in a school if they had allowed it back then. I am glad my daddy taught me how to be a man, and not just any old man. I'm a smart man and going to have some smart children, too! I pray for my future! The dreams I've asked God to show me, I believe He's going to do just what I asked of Him," William said as he looked Sarah in her eyes.

Sarah smiled. She had never felt so happy inside. *"Momma, you were right! Everything you told me about a man is true. I feel good, Momma! I think this is the man for me if he will have me! I don't know how to love, but I can learn with God's help. God, please don't let him get away from me. Show me that he's the one,"* she thought.

William looked out the window, and asked, "Where did you say you were going?" He startled Sarah, who was lost in thought, gazing out the window. She quickly gathered her thoughts and said, "Oh, I'm going to Forsyth County!" William looked at Sarah with a smile on his face and said, "That's a coincidence. I'm going there too!"

The train conductor yelled, "Next stop, the town of Winston-Salem." Sarah grabbed her bag and waited for William to let her out. "Where are you staying, Sarah?" he asked. Sarah walked to the front of the train and turned around. "I don't know yet. I'm going to wait at the station and ask someone about a room." Luckily, William knew how to get information about rooms for rent and other resources for shelter. He read in the newspaper that there was a hotel boarding house on Main Street. "Sarah, I have this paper, and if you would like, we can search together and get a room. Let's sit here and see what we can find.

Look at this: 'One bedroom for rent. 50 cents a week. Clean bathroom and stove.' Here is another one: 'One bedroom. Front window view. Bathroom and stove for 75 cents a week.' And there are several boarding homes in the uptown area. Do you want to look at some of these places?" Sarah was tired and wanted to take a nap. It had been a long day on the train. She agreed to look at the room that was 50 cents a week.

William and Sarah walked about four blocks on Main Street. "There's the building," said William. They entered and asked the clerk if there were any vacant rooms available. The clerk motioned for them to go on the other street where the Negroes lived, and said, "We don't rent to coloreds here. They have their own rooms for rent to their own kind. If you can't find anything there, check with some of the residents. They will give you somewhere to stay for the night." They thanked the clerk and went their way.

Sarah was getting tired. They had walked for several blocks and were getting hungry. William noticed that a light was on at one of the homes nearby. "This is all coloreds on this side of town. Let's stop here and ask someone for directions. If they don't rent, maybe they know someone who will!" William walked to the house first and knocked on the door. A small-framed woman opened the door and said, "Hello Sir, may I help you?" William removed his hat and said, "Yes, ma'am. My friend and I are looking for somewhere to stay for the night. We've been looking all evening, and we are tired and need to sleep. Do you have any vacant rooms for rent?" The woman shined the candle in his face and asked, "Are you two married?" William didn't know what to say at first, so he told the truth. "No, Ma'am. I was helping her find a place until tomorrow. I can sleep mostly anywhere. If you have a room, she can pay for it and I will come back tomorrow and get her." The woman opened the door so they could come in. "Well, since you two are not married, I can let you have a room on the other side of the house. It's not much, but you won't be outside in the cold. The room is 25 cents a week. You buy your own food. The bathroom is outside and there's a slop jar in each room. You make sure you empty it each morning and wash it out. There are clean sheets and blankets on the bed. Lights must be out at 12 midnight or before. Come with me, young lady, and you sir, you can go to the back room near the kitchen," the woman said. William told Sarah everything was going to be alright. The woman directed him to his room.

She looked at Sarah and said, "You're a pretty little thing. What are you doing with a man and not married? He's good to look at! Are you engaged?" Sarah folded her arms around her bag and replied, "No. We just met on the train. I'm only 24. I've never had a boyfriend. He's been a big help to me. I suppose you can say we are just friends." The woman directed Sarah to her bedroom, and said, "Well, I tell you. You better think about getting him for your boyfriend before these gals in Winston-Salem get a sniff of him. They will take him away from you so fast, you would think somebody kidnapped him. When you two walked in my house, I thought you were a couple. My eyes sure fooled me that time. The Lord shows me things. I trust what He shows me, and He is showing me that—what's his name?" Sarah answered, "William."

The woman continued. "That's your husband! I can feel it in my bones. You two don't act like most of the people I meet around here. It's something different about that young man, and you, too. You were raised by good people. Couldn't you tell by the way he didn't lie about you? Most men would have said, 'Yes! That's my old lady' just to go to bed with you. But he didn't. He respects you like a man should. You take it from an old woman like me. Do you like him?" she asked. Sarah paused. "I can tell that you do by the way you didn't answer right off. I'm going to tell you what to do. Play hard to get. If you don't find a place to stay tomorrow, come back here, and I'll rent you a room. You can stay long as you want to. Let him find his own place, and if he comes back to see how you're doing, you got him! Listen to your heart, baby! God will direct your path. You go on and get washed up for bed. We can talk more tomorrow," the woman said. Sarah thanked her and pondered all that she heard in her heart.

As Sarah walked down the hallway of the large cottage-style farmhouse, she turned and asked, "You know ma'am, I'm sorry, what is your name?" The woman smiled at Sarah and said, "You can call me Miss Nelson."

CHAPTER 2

•••

The next morning, Sarah got up bright and early. Saturdays were a good day to search for a room. She asked Miss Nelson for directions to the best and cheapest apartments in town. Miss Nelson walked to the front door with Sarah. She opened the door, pointed to Main Street and said, "You get on the street across town, which is Main Street. Walk about three blocks and you will be on Old Salem Road. That's a new development for us. If you go any further, you will run into the White folks' section." Sarah thanked her and started on her journey. As she walked down the street, Miss Nelson yelled at her and said, "You be careful and remember what I said."

Sarah walked for about two miles around town. She stopped to rest near an old vegetable stand. There was a man standing under the shed selling vegetables. Sarah decided to stop for a while. "Hello, Sir! Sir, excuse me, please." The man turned and looked at her, and asked, "What do you want young lady? If you're looking for work, I can't help you. So, what can I do for you?" Sarah looked perplexed and said, "All I want is a cup of water, please." He reached under his homemade table and said, "Well now, I think I can spare a cup of water." He poured Sarah a cup of water and offered her a seat on one of his chairs. While she was resting, someone walked up behind her and touched her on the shoulder. "I thought that was you. How you're doing this morning and how did you sleep last night?" a man asked. When she turned around, it was William. He was also out looking for a place to live. "William, I didn't know you would be out this early in the morning. Have you had any luck?" she asked.

"I found a place and was blessed to find a job, too! I went to the new site where they are building a college. They're tearing down the school, and a man I met in town last night told me to be down there at 6 a.m. I got up praying to the Lord that someone would hire me. And you know another thing? When I went to ask about the job, the head man asked me where I was living. I told him I was looking for a place. He told me to go to a neighborhood called, Old Salem. It's not too far from here. Do you want to go with me?" he asked Sarah. "Well, I haven't had any luck on my own, so I might as well go with you," she said. The two of them walked together down Main Street, hoping to get a place to live soon.

After walking for about an hour, William saw a sign that read "Apartment for Rent." As they neared the building, Sarah noticed that there were only one bedroom apartments available. They walked into the office of the building. A White man was sitting at a desk. "Hello sir," said William. "I read on the sign in the window that you have an apartment for rent. By any chance, do you have two?" The man looked at William and asked, "What you need with two apartments? You and your wife don't look old enough to have grown children. You two are married, aren't you?" William looked at Sarah. He had to catch his breath before speaking. All at once, he let it out. "We are engaged to be married, if she will have me."

Sarah's eyes began to mist. She had to take a deep breath. Her heart was filled with joy. "Yes, I'll have you, Mr. William Clingman. I would be honored to be your wife!" The man told them that they could get the apartment. "When is the big day?" he asked William. Sarah looked at William to see what he would say. "There's a lot of things I need to do before I set a date. I need to start working, first. What good would I be to my wife without a job? I have never told anyone this, Sir, but the first time I laid my eyes on this lady standing here, I knew that God was in the midst of it all. I felt in my soul that she was the woman for me. She's the prettiest woman I have ever seen on God's green Earth...besides my momma," he said with a smile while looking into Sarah's eyes. William hugged Sarah and kissed her forehead.

The man told them that the apartment would be ready the following week. Before William agreed to get the apartment, he turned to Sarah, got down on one knee and asked her would she be his wife. Sarah nodded as tears ran down her cheeks. The two left the office holding hands, excited about their engagement. Sarah couldn't wait to tell Miss Nelson the good news.

Later that evening, Sarah and William stopped to get something to eat. The Old Tavern Café was open. Sarah noticed that a sign was in the window that read, "Help Needed. Looking for a great cook five days a week. $2.50 a week. Inquire inside."

"Look, William. Let's stop here. I'm going to ask about the job they have in the window," said Sarah. William agreed as he thought this would also be a good place to order dinner. As they stood at the counter, Sarah asked the owner about the job that was posted. A tall White man told her that he needed someone who could cook and clean. "If you want the job young lady, you have to talk to my wife. She does all the hiring around here. I tell you what! When I get your food ready, you can go outside this door. I live in the next house. There's a path next to this place that leads to the back porch. I'll send word that you are coming," the man said. Sarah was happy that William stopped for dinner. William and Sarah stood outside the building as they waited for their food. A boy brought their food to them, and said, "That will be 25 cents, Sir."

William paid the boy and Sarah walked to the back door of the house. She knocked on the screen door. A small, frail-looking woman came to the door. "May I help you, Honey?" she asked. Sarah told her that she was looking for work and wanted to apply for the job in the window. She asked Sarah and William to come in. "That job only pays $2.50 a week. You need to be in the kitchen at 6 a.m. and leave at 5 p.m. You get your pay on Fridays. Are you and your husband from this area?" she asked. William looked at Sarah, and said, "No Ma'am. We are from Virginia! We moved to North Carolina this week. We hope to have a family one day and make Winston-Salem our home," said William, as he looked at Sarah with a smile.

"You seem to be a nice couple. I don't know of anyone who lives in Virginia, but if they are as nice as you two, Virginia is a good place to be from! You come back Monday morning bright and early. I'll let my husband know that you will be here. By the way, can you cook?" the woman asked. Sarah told her yes, and that she knew how to clean a house too! "Good night to you both, and I'll see you Monday morning," said the woman.

CHAPTER 3

...

Sunday was going to be sleep-in day for Sarah. The only thing she could think about was William getting down on his knee to propose to her. As she turned over in that big, comfortable bed she was lying in, she heard a soft knock at the door. It was Miss Nelson. "Come in," said Sarah. Miss Nelson peeped in the door, and asked, "Are you sleeping, my dear?" Sarah shook her head and invited her in. "I want to know how your day went yesterday. I was in bed when you came home last night," said Miss Nelson.

Sarah sat up on the side of the bed and began telling her about the apartment and her job. "You know, Miss Nelson! I am so happy. I have had a hard time in my life. But I feel so blessed to have met William and now you! I never thought in a million years I would be here in North

Carolina, looking for a job and an apartment to live in. God has truly blessed me to meet William. Do you know what happened last evening?" Sarah asked.

Miss Nelson looked so excited. "He proposed to me! We were standing in the café and he got down on his knee and proposed!" she said, as she held Miss Nelson's hands. "Baby, I told you there was something good in that man. The Lord has never fooled me to be wrong about stuff like that. I have been in the world a long time. I've seen men come and go. The bad ones always talking under a woman's dress. The good ones want to buy a woman a dress! There's a difference there!" she said. "You will get it if you live long enough. But let me get back to you and William! Did you accept?" she asked. Sarah paused for a minute and said, "Of course, I did! I think I fell in love with him on the train. It was something about how he looked at me and treated me as though I was his woman. I don't believe the Lord would lead me to a man who was not for me. Momma always told me, 'If you ask and don't faint, God will answer your prayers.'"

Miss Nelson said, "Your momma told you right! A real Christian mother won't lead her children in the wrong path. I don't know your mother, and I have just met you, but God knows us all. I can feel it in my bones! You and William are going to do well in this county. You didn't tell me if you found a job yet." Sarah gave Miss Nelson a piece of paper with the store owner's name on it, and said, "Yes!

William will be working at the site where the college is being built and I got a job at the café where he proposed to me. The owner's wife was excited to have a cook on duty." Miss Nelson hugged Sarah and told her she was proud of her and William. "I would like to stay here for a few months if you don't mind. I'm working now and I can pay what you ask!" said Sarah. Miss Nelson thought for a moment and said, "I tell you what! Why don't you wait until a month from now to pay rent! I want you and William to get on your feet and start your life with a little something in your pocket. By the way, have you decided on a date, yet?"

Sarah didn't answer. She wanted to wait until Willian was present. "I want us both to set a date! He might want a long engagement and I don't want to go too fast." Miss Nelson stood in the doorway and said, "There're ways a woman can make him marry next month!" Then she smiled and closed the door.

A few hours later, Sarah got up and took a bath. She unpacked her bag and took out one of her nicer dresses. She wanted to walk around town and see the buildings, the other stores in town and find a nice church to attend. When she finished dressing, she saw William through the front room window. She ran to open the door. As he walked in, he gave Sarah a hug and kissed her forehead. "I wanted to tell you more last night, but it was getting late. I love you, Sarah Clingman, with all my heart. I want to be your husband. I will try so hard to be the best husband a woman could ask for. I asked God to send me the perfect woman for me. And when I saw you for the first time, I knew it was God! My heart was all in it! I was afraid to move when we were on the train. I thought, if I moved, you would get away from me. So, I let you in to sit by my side. Now, the question is, when do you want to get married? I'm not rushing you! I want to have a month, a year, or days in my mind. Please don't say a year," he said, as he hugged her tightly in his arms.

Sarah didn't know what to say. Tears rolled down her cheeks. William tenderly held her face in his hands and wiped her tears away. "William Clingman, it would be my honor to be your wife. I'm not perfect, but I do love you in my heart and in my mind. I can't think of anyone else I want to live the rest of my life with. I prayed to God to send me a man with dignity, pride, strength and most of all God-fearing. I would marry you tomorrow, but we have much work to do before we can make any plans. Before you came by, I was going to walk around town to see if there was a church in this area. We need to attend God's house on Sundays. Would you like to walk with me? Maybe we can ask some of the neighbors to direct us," she said.

William agreed to go with Sarah. On their way through town, they saw a man sitting on a bench near one of the stores. William approached the man, and said,

"Howdy, Sir. My name is William Clingman. Me and my wife-to-be are looking for a good church to attend. Do you know of any nearby?"

The man looked at William, then he looked at Sarah and said, "Howdy to both of you! So, you are the people I heard about. They say you are new to this area. Now, I tell you. If you want to go to a church, there's about three nearby. If you want to worship my Lord and Savior, get into the good Word and gospel of Jesus, you need to come to my church, The Church of Christ. It's not too far from here!"

The man reached out his hand to William and said, "Robert Dockery is my name, but everybody around here calls me 'Doc.' You don't have to be fancy and all of that! I'm just a man who loves the Lord and wants to live right before my God. You say this here is your wife-to-be? She's a mighty pretty thing, and you ain't bad looking yourself! Take it from this old man, don't look any further. Come join me and my family next Sunday. We start service at 10 a.m. and Wednesday Night Bible service at 7 p.m. It's been my pleasure meeting you. By the way, can you read boy?"

William smiled at Mr. Dockery and said, "Yes, sir. I've been halfway around the world! I served my country for more than two years, sir, but I learned to read and write as a young child. I can remember so well. My grandma was a slave on a plantation in South Carolina. She told us stories about how one man taught them how to read the Bible first, then, how to write and read their names. My daddy was smart enough to read and write. He taught all his children to read, and we learned to write at an early age. So, if anyone in your church has any problems reading, I will be more than happy to teach them." The two men said their goodbyes. William and Sarah walked around town. Sarah wanted to go by the café to get something to eat.

After dinner, William walked with Sarah back to her room. Miss Nelson stood in the doorway. As she opened the door for Sarah, she called at William and asked, "Have you set the date yet?" William smiled and said, "It won't be long!" He tipped his hat and hugged Sarah goodbye.

Miss Nelson was eager to know what their plans were. She couldn't wait for Sarah to come inside. "Come on in here and talk to me child. Did you find a church?" asked Miss Nelson. Sarah sat on the sofa and shared the good news. "We met a nice gentleman on our way in town. A Mr. Dockery, I believe to be his name. He invited William and me to come to his church. He said that his congregation is small and some of the members have a problem with reading. William offered to help with anything needed. I think it will be a nice start for us," said Sarah.

Miss Nelson was so happy to hear the news. "Well, tell me this! Have you set a date to get hitched?" Sarah paused for a minute and said, "I think it will be this year.

Maybe in a few more months. I'm 24 now and would like to start a family soon, but we'll see! William and I need to work more and save for our future. I'll start my job next week and William will start tomorrow. I feel so happy. I prayed to God for this day. He will direct our paths." Miss Nelson hugged Sarah and gave her blessing for their marriage.

It was getting late, and Sarah had to get up early to meet the lady at the café. She went to the kitchen to heat her bath water. While she waited for the water to heat, she sat down at the table and thought about her mother. Tears flowed down her face and said to herself, *"Momma, I loved you so much. You told me that one day I would find the love of my life. I think William is it! He's everything a woman would want from a man. I don't think God is leading me wrong. I trusted him when you were sick. We didn't have much, but God took care of us. He didn't let you suffer long. He kept you by my side until I was able to do for myself. I'm going to keep on trusting him with my life. If you agree with my decision, show me somehow with your sweet spirit, Momma. Come to me like you have many times before. I need your spiritual guidance."*

Sarah got up and wiped her tears. The water was hot and ready to pour in the basin. She bathed and put on her gown. Before she knelt to say her prayers, she heard a soft knock at the door. "Come in!" she said. It was Miss Nelson. "Sarah, before you go to sleep, I want you to read something for me. It's a verse in my Bible. I read it every night before I go to sleep, and the Lord will always answer your prayers. He may not answer when you want him too, but he will answer. Here, take this book and read it. I'll get it tomorrow morning."

Sarah took the Bible and opened it to the book Miss Nelson had folded. She began to read aloud. *"Show me the right path, O Lord; point out the road for me to follow. Lead me by your truth and teach me, for you are the God who saves me. All day long I put my hope in you. Remember, O Lord, your compassion and unfailing love, which you have shown from long ages past. Oh my God. Psalm 25:4-6. Thank you, Momma. Thank you, Holy Spirit!"* Sarah turned her bed covers back, fell on her knees, and praised God for sending his Holy Spirit.

CHAPTER 4

...

Sarah got up early Monday morning. She wanted to be at the café before 6 a.m. The walk there was only about 30 minutes. She arrived at 5:30 a.m. As she walked to the door, the old woman greeted her and asked her to come in. "Come on in, young lady. I want to show you where the kitchen is. By the way, did I tell you my name?" Sarah shook her head and the lady said, "You can call me Mrs. Griffin and my husband is Mr. Griffin! I expect you to keep this area clean during the day. Wash the dishes every time you take them from the table. The menus are on the wall and make sure you have enough wood to keep the fire burning. Come with me. I want you to meet Miss Sue. She is the clerk and waitress. She will give you the orders and you prepare the meals. Oh yes, make sure the coffee pot stays hot all day long."

Sarah thanked Mrs. Griffin for showing her around the kitchen. She found an apron in the broom closet. There was a bonnet for her hair. No one needed to train Sarah for her job. She knew what to do and how it was to be done.

At 8 a.m., Miss Sue walked in the kitchen to talk to Sarah. She had an order slip in her hand, and asked, "Can you read this, Sarah? Mrs. Griffin didn't tell me much about you. Most of the help can't read in this part of town." She held the slip of paper in Sarah's face, and said, "What's this say?" Sarah didn't know what part of the paper she was referring to, so she started reading, "Date, time, customer's name, coffee, grits, eggs, bacon, toast, cheese, hot cakes, oatmeal, orange."

"STOP! So, you can read! Who taught you to read?" Miss Sue asked Sarah. Sarah turned her back to Miss Sue and said, "My momma taught me to read and write. Never judge a book by the cover, I was told as a child." Miss Sue was stunned. She knew Negroes who didn't know how to read their names, but Sarah was amazing. "Can I ask you something else, Sarah? Where are you from? Because you don't look like the other Negroes around here. Are you from across the water, like you see in the magazines?" Miss Sue asked.

Sarah looked at her and smiled, answering, "No! I'm from Virginia. I was born in Canada. I was raised by my mother and grandmother. Is there something else you would like to know about me? I should be working, not socializing." Miss Sue watched as Sarah prepared the next order. Everything was neat and clean in the kitchen. Sarah had her first break at 11 a.m.

By noon, the café was crowded. People can from everywhere! Some of the orders were for the workers who were building the new college dorms. Miss Sue served the customers in the front and Sarah served the back door orders. She enjoyed seeing new faces and meeting new people. They were thankful to have someone as nice as Sarah serving them.

At closing time, Sarah was ready to go home. She took off her apron and bonnet. The kitchen was clean, and the stove was cooling. Mrs. Griffin walked through the kitchen for inspection. "Well, Sarah! I think you are going to work out fine! Everything looks good in here! The customers were pleased with their meal. You be back here at 6 a.m. You may go now," she said.

As Sarah walked down the street, she saw William coming across the street. As he approached her, he said, "How did your day go?" Sarah greeted him with a hug and said, "I had a good day! I think I'm going to like my job! I got a chance to meet some new people on this side of town. Several of them go to the church where we were invited. My feet are killing me! I can't wait to put them in some hot water. Are you coming by tonight?" she asked.

He stared into Sarah's eyes, and said, "I love you, Sarah. I don't want to stay apart from you. I need you every night and day. Let's not wait too long to get married. We can stay in my apartment until we work and save enough money to get something bigger. It will be alright. I prayed and asked God to bless us, be with us and I know he will do what he said he will do. Let's trust God with our marriage. Next week is the second week in February. What about getting married on that Sunday?" Sarah smiled and gave William a hug and said, "Yes! We can marry next Sunday!" William yelled as loud as he could, "Yes! She said yes!"

They walked down the street holding hands. William made plans to buy a new suit. He had to talk to the pastor of the church. He didn't have to worry about inviting guests, because they didn't know anyone except the Griffins, Miss Nelson, and the men on his job.

This was going to be the biggest thing happening on that side of town.

CHAPTER 5

•••

When Sarah arrived at her room, Miss Nelson was standing in the doorway holding the door open. "Come on in, baby! I know you are tired. I filled the kettle with water. It's hot and ready for those feet! How was your day?" she asked. Sarah walked in and greeted Miss Nelson. "I had a great day. I saw some new faces today and learned a lot about who I'm working with."

Miss Nelson interrupted and said, "Let me tell you about some of those people you work for! Don't you tell them any of your business! If they ask you about your personal life, act like you don't hear them. I know all about the Griffins. They are nice and they are good people, but your business ain't everybody's business. Take it from me, baby. Don't tell them nothing, because they're not going to tell you nothing, but what they want you to know—and that's nothing. I'm an old woman. I know what I'm talking about! Now, keep on talking, child!"

Sarah sat on the side of the bed. She motioned for Miss Nelson to sit too. "I have something to ask of you. I would like to know if you would help me get ready for my wedding?" Tears streamed down Miss Nelson's face. "Oh my Lord, child. I prayed for God to let you know it was time. He has answered my prayer! Yes Lord! I'm ready for anything you want me to do. You need a dress! I'll buy you one. Need shoes! I'll get them too. You know what, Honey! The Lord sent you here. He sent you to me. I had all boys and always wanted a girl. He knew you were coming to be in my life! Thank you, Jesus! Now, when's the wedding?"

Sarah hugged Miss Nelson and said, "William and I set the date for next week. Do you think you will have enough time?" Miss Nelson was overjoyed. She said, "You know what next week is? Valentine's! The perfect time to show your love. My papa taught me a poem many years ago. Do you want to hear it? It's perfect for this moment." Sarah nodded.

"The rose is red, the violet's blue.
The honey is sweet, and so are you.
Thou art my love and I am thine;
I drew thee to my Valentine:
The lot was cast and then I drew, and
Fortune said it should be you."

Sarah's eyes glistened like the stars shining on a sky blue night. She washed herself and got ready for bed. When she kneeled to pray, she asked the Lord to bless her wedding day and all those who were willing to help her.

This week was going to be stressful. Sarah had to go by the church to talk with the pastor. She was to meet William after 5 p.m. She told Mrs. Griffin about the wedding plans and invited her and Mr. Griffin to attend.

Miss Nelson ordered flowers for the church and called the pastor for rehearsal on Friday. Everything was set to go, except one thing—rings for the bride and groom. She knew the jeweler in town, so she decided to go by the store and tell him about the wedding. She knew that William could get a set of rings on credit, since they both were working. If she needed to, she was willing to stand for whatever they bought.

Later that evening, she couldn't wait to tell Sarah about what she had done. When Sarah walked into the house, Miss Nelson told her about the dress, the flowers, rehearsal, and the rings. "Miss Nelson, you are a sweetheart! I don't know if I could have done any of this without your help. And the rings...I didn't have rings on my mind. We will make all of this up to you. William is coming over later this evening. We will sit down and tell him about the plans. He was supposed to talk to the pastor today. I hope he'll let us have it at the church," said Sarah.

William arrived with good news. "The pastor is excited about the wedding date. And you Miss Nelson, I thank you for all your help. You have been a God-sent angel in our life." Sarah looked at William and said, "Honey, you know one thing we forgot? Rings!" William's mouth dropped open and said, "Oh my! What are we going to do?" Miss Nelson looked at him and said, "Don't worry about the rings. I know the man who owns the jewelry store in town. He will let you pick out the rings on credit. I've already told him about you, and if you and Sarah get in a bind, I will be there to help you out. I love you two just that much!"

CHAPTER 6

...

Saturday, February 13, 1896

Sarah worked a full week and earned her first $2.50. She was proud of herself. She put her money in a small change purse. Mrs. Griffin was so thankful for Sarah. Their business had doubled in one week with Sarah working there. "Sarah, I want you to know how thankful I am for you. My store has never had this much business. We will be honored to attend your wedding tomorrow. And, another thing, my husband decided to give you a week's pay for your wedding gift. Here is another $2.50. Bless you on your wedding day." Sarah didn't know what to say. "Mrs. Griffin. I am willing to work extra hours next week. You don't know what this means to me and my husband. May God bless you for doing this for us! I promise you! I will work harder, from now on."

After work, Sarah walked home. She was excited about her wedding day. When she arrived, Miss Nelson was waiting for her to try on the dress. "Come on in the house, baby! I know you are tired, so go in there and rest yourself a bit. Are you hungry? I made a sweet potato pie and some greens on the stove. I'm going to my room. You call me if you need help with your dress," she said.

Sarah opened the box. The dress was in a plastic cover. She removed the cover and to her delight, inside there was a beautiful white dress with pearls around the neck and sleeves. There was lace around the hem and a train made of satin ribbons. She could not believe her eyes. "Oh my God. What in the world!? I have never seen such a beautiful dress as this!" She began taking off her clothes and yelled for Miss Nelson to come.

Miss Nelson rushed to the bedroom and Sarah had the dress in front of her as she stood in the mirror. "It is beautiful, Miss Nelson. I can't believe this is happening to me." Miss Nelson stood back and watched Sarah as she paraded back and forth. "Well, let's try it on!" said Miss Nelson.

Sarah undressed and stepped into her wedding dress. Miss Nelson carefully zipped her up. "Perfect! You look like a queen! Try your shoes on with the dress. That William won't know you tomorrow. Now, turn around, baby. Oh, my stars! A picture in a book! That's what you are.

I have had this dress for more than 10 years. I bought it from a salesman who came through here from Paris. I thought, maybe one day I would have a daughter of my own, but it didn't happen, So, I saved it! I was going to sell it one time, but something told me to wait, and I'm glad something did!" Sarah leaned over and kissed Miss Nelson on her cheek. "I am proud to wear your dress, Miss Nelson. I know I'm not your blood daughter, but I will love you like I'm your own flesh and blood, said Sarah. Sarah took the dress off with Miss Nelson's help. She put it in the plastic cover and placed it back into the box.

Later that evening, William came over with good news. "Everything is set! I have the rings and we are to be at the church in an hour for rehearsal. Miss Nelson, I would like to thank you for all you have done for me and my wife-to-be." As William sat down, tears rolled down his face and he began to pour out his heart to Miss Nelson. "You know, when we first came to this city, I had no idea that the people would welcome us so warmly. This is the way God wants his people to live. I'm grateful this evening, knowing that I have found true friends in this neighbor. I know that there will be many who will not feel the same way about us, but anything that me and my wife can do for you and anyone else, just let us know." He stood and hugged Miss Nelson.

CHAPTER 7

•••

Sunday, February 14, 1896

Sunday morning was going to be busy. Sarah got up early to get a fresh start. Miss Nelson prepared breakfast. She laid her best Sunday suit out on the bed. Her shoes were in the closet with all the other accessories. She went down the hallway to Sarah's room and knocked on the door. "Sarah, are you up, baby? I want you to put my hair in a ball after I get dressed." Sarah opened the door, and said, "Sure, I'll be glad to help you. Let me help you with those buttons. You look like a queen yourself. Are you sure I'm the girl who is getting married?" she asked with a smile. The two ladies enjoyed getting ready for the wedding.

It was now 10 a.m. The wedding would start in only

four hours! Miss Nelson cleaned her kitchen, and filled the kettles with water. She added more wood to the stove so the water would get hotter.

Around noon, Sarah and Miss Nelson gathered everything and headed to the church. When they arrived, everyone was in place. Sarah went to the dressing room where Mrs. Griffin and several other ladies of the church were ready to help. "Come on in, ladies," said Mrs. Griffin. Miss Nelson and two other sisters helped Sarah with her dress.

"Oh, my Lord! You look like an angel from Heaven. That dress in gorgeous on you. It looks as if it was made just for you," said Mrs. Griffin. Sarah looked in the mirror. She turned from side to side, looking at how beautiful she was. "How should I wear my hair, up or down on my shoulders?" asked Sarah. The women observed Sarah and gave their opinion. "I think it would look beautiful on your shoulders," said Miss Nelson, holding back tears. Sarah turned and noticed Miss Nelson was crying. "Don't cry, Miss Nelson! I know what you are thinking! It will be alright. I feel like this is your day, too. Be happy for me. If you cry, I will cry too, and we can't have that," said Sarah. "These are tears of joy," said Miss Nelson. Everyone agreed, as they dried their own tears and fixed their makeup.

The little church was decorated with flowers and wedding bells. The pastor waited at the altar. Mr. and

Mrs. Griffin stood to give the bride away. William came from the back to stand with the Griffins. Everyone else was seated in their proper place. The pianist played soft music for the occasion.

The ushers opened the door and Sarah waked in. As she walked slowly down the aisle, William looked at the woman who God promised for him. He couldn't believe his eyes. She was the most beautiful woman he ever saw. Sarah didn't stop until she reached the pastor's hand. William and Sarah joined hands in prayer.

Mr. and Mrs. William Clingman enjoyed a Holy Feast on the church's campground. Everyone brought baskets filled with their favorite dishes. One of the brothers of the church brought a small bottle of wine. He called for everyone's attention and yelled. "Hear ye, hear ye. All God's people! Listen up! In my Bible, it says, 'Don't drink only water. You ought to drink a little wine for the sake of your stomach because you are sick so often.' Now, it said a little wine. So, if you don't believe me, read for yourself. 1 Timothy 5:23. I have this small bottle of wine to celebrate the marriage of this fine couple. Here, take a cup and pour yourselves a little bit and let us drink to the husband and wife." Everyone at the campground took a cup, poured a little wine, and drank in Jesus' name.

CHAPTER 8

•••

William and Sarah were busy working together to save money for their new home. Sarah bought several items and kept them at Miss Nelson's home. People from all over the neighborhood heard about the wedding. They bought gifts and collected money from all the merchants in that area.

William was earning more money on his job. The company he worked for showed their appreciation by giving him $7 a day! He was making enough to pay rent, buy food, and pay on his rings at the jewelry store.

Finally, it was moving day. Sarah and William moved early one Saturday morning to their new home. They borrowed a mule and buggy from one of their friends from church. Sarah packed all their gifts, clothes, and work equipment.

William was introduced to a co-worker on his job. He had some used furniture that he wanted to give away. His friend agreed to leave everything in his barn until William was married. It would be a nice surprise for Sarah. "Honey, we have to turn around and go the other way. I forget something," he told Sarah. He began to turn the wagon around and Sarah asked, "What did you forget?" William continued to go in a different direction and answered, "Well, I have a little surprise for you. Have you noticed, we are moving, but we don't have a bed to sleep on and a stove for cooking?" Sarah looked puzzled, and said, "You know, when you are in love, you don't think about stuff like that. I thought, maybe we can make a pallet on the floor and sleep on my quilts. It doesn't matter to me, as long as we are together. So, where are we going?" William smiled and let his surprise out. "I have furniture! One of the workers on the job heard about us getting married. He had some used furniture in his shed and offered it to me. I was quick to say 'yes!' I hope you don't mind. We can clean it up and use it until we can buy our own, brand new from the store." Sarah hugged her new husband and said, "If you say it's alright, then it's alright."

William loaded the furniture on the wagon. His friend gave them enough furniture to furnish their entire home. They had a kitchen table with two chairs, an ice box to store food and other items, a sofa and two chairs for their living room, and a full-sized feather mattress with log cabin style headboard. Everything they needed to start housekeeping was loaded on the wagon.

The population of Lewisville, North Carolina was 7% Negro families. William and Sarah rode until they found the street they were moving to. "This looks like it right here. Lucy Lane! There's the house on the right. It's okay for a start. I can do some repairing on my own. It won't take much to get it the way you want it. I think we have enough money to buy material for our curtains. When you get finished with this house, it will look different. I know you can make anything look better and feel better, too," he said as he smiled at Sarah.

By the time evening came, everything was in the house. Sarah had all their wedding gifts packed in one box. "Let's go through the gifts and see what we have. I don't want to buy the same things at the store," she said. As she began opening the box, she saw that one of the women at the church had given her a roll of material. It was enough to make curtains for all the windows and a spread for her bed. She also had several tin drinking cups and pans to match. There were pots and pans for cooking. There was a small flat box wrapped in a fine velvet covering. She opened it. Miss Nelson's name was on the inside lid. It was a six-piece flatware set. "Oh my God! This is too beautiful to use! I bet she paid a lot of money for this. I didn't see her when she brought it out. You know William, God has truly blessed us. Nobody did it

but God," said Sarah. "I can remember when we boarded the train. I didn't have anything but my little bag on
my lap. And, you didn't know where you were going. But
look at us now! We may not be rich, but we have everything we need. I thank God for you, William. I'm going
to make you one of the happiest men on this side of Winston-Salem, North Carolina."

William walked into their sitting room and began to
pray. He held Sarah's hand and looked toward Heaven
and prayed, *"Father God. We come together to give you
all the praise and honor because it belongs to you and no
other. I want to thank you Lord for taking care of us. We
have been on this journey for a longtime, but You, Oh God,
have never left us nor forsaken us. You and You alone are
the hope we long for. In my youth, I put my trust in You,
Father. Be with me and my wife and bless our home. Thank
You God for all our friends and loved ones. Bless their families. Bless the church and members who blessed us with
gifts that were so much needed for our home. You also said
in Your Word, 'For whosoever shall give you a cup of water
to drink in my name, because you belong to Me, verily I say
unto you, they shall not lose their reward. Not only did they
give us water and food to eat, but they also gave us their
love. Pour out Your blessings on each one of them, Father,
and never take Your hands off us. In Jesus' Name, I pray.
Amen!"*

After getting everything off the wagon, Sarah cut material for her curtains. William cleaned the floors and put their bed together. All the furniture was put in its proper place. It seemed as if everything was done within no time.

Later that night, Sarah placed their clothes in a wooden chest that was at the foot of their bed. "I hope we will be able to buy another chest soon. I need one more for you and one for our guests." William looked back at her and asked, "Are we going to have guests staying overnight?" Sarah didn't hesitate to answer, "Yes. I would love for Miss Nelson to come stay for a while. Not now! But maybe later this Spring. It would be good for her to leave town and come to the countryside." William agreed with his wife and said, "I think that would be a great idea."

CHAPTER 9

...

Early Monday morning, William and Sarah rode the mule and buggy to work. It was colder than usual. The clouds appeared white and puffy. "I hope we don't get any snow before the end of the month. We need more quilts and another heater for the bedroom. But what can we do about the weather? God has been with us through many storms, and I know He will be with us with the storm ahead of us," William said. Sarah's teeth chattered as the wind blew under her scarf. She buried herself deeply under William's arm for warmth.

...

The café was ready for customers. Sarah cooked the breakfast meals and Miss Sue collected the orders. "How was the wedding, if I may ask?" said Miss Sue. Sarah kept working as she answered. "My husband and I had a beautiful wedding day! We received many nice gifts from our friends and church members. We moved into our home the other day. There's still a lot of work to be done," Sarah said, while making the biscuits and preparing the plates for serving.

The two women worked at a steady pace. Sarah added coal to the stove every hour. She chopped the vegetables for lunch. "Bubble and Squeak will be on the menu today!" she said. Miss Sue stood by watching. "What is that?" asked Miss Sue. Sarah continued to chop the vegetables and beef from the leftover meal from Sunday. "It's a dish my momma made for us when I was a child. It's very good, and you don't waste food. 'Use the leftovers,' she would tell me. I want you to taste it when I'm done," she said. Sarah continued to make lunch while Miss Sue watched. She added fat drippings to the vegetables and gathered the breadcrumbs for the dressing. She peeled the potatoes and chopped them with a knife. The gravy was made, and the meal was completed. "Come over here, Miss Sue, and taste this new dish." Miss Sue got a plate and spoon. She dipped the serving spoon into the pot, and said, "Oh my! This is good. I have never tasted anything like this before. How long have you been cooking like this?" Sarah smiled and added, "I started cooking when I was 12 years old. I watched my momma. You know what Miss Sue? You can learn a lot about things when you have your heart in it. God gave all of us a mind. It's up to us to do right or wrong. When you do right, you will listen and obey. When you do wrong, you turn your back away from right. I decided to do right because my momma told me it would serve me well someday. Now, you see! What I learned from my momma is helping me make a decent living for me and my husband. Obedience will pay off!" Sarah said.

Mrs. Griffin watched as the customers filled her café. Not a table was vacant. Everyone was commenting on the good food. They wanted to know who the new cook was. Mrs. Griffin made more money in one day than she did all week before. She went into the kitchen with Sarah. "I want to thank you, Sarah. That meal you cooked was the best we have had in a long time. All my customers are well-pleased. If you want to make another one of your favorite dishes, you just help yourself. I'm going to turn the kitchen over to you." Sarah thanked Mrs. Griffin. She finished cleaning the kitchen and prepared for the dinner menu.

5 p.m. didn't come soon enough. William was waiting outside the café. When he saw Sarah, he jumped off the wagon seat to help his wife on. Sarah needed to get a few things from the local general store. "Could we please stop in the general store so I can look around? I need a few items for the house," said Sarah. William agreed.

He entered the store with her. As he was exploring the aisles, he saw a box with a toy train on it. He picked up the box, looked at the cover and asked the clerk, "How much is this train, Sir?" The clerk told him it was on sale for 75 cents. He walked over to William and said, "That's one of the new toys I ordered. I hope they will sell at that price. Most of my customers can't afford toys like this, especially right after Christmas."

"I'll take it, if you let me have it on credit!" said William. The clerk said he could get it for 25 cents down and 25 cents a month. William took the train and placed it in the back of the buggy. He went back inside the store to wait for Sarah. Sarah was at the counter with everything she needed. "Would you like for me to put these on a charge ticket for you, Sarah?" asked the clerk. She said, "Yes! and look for us on the first of the month to pay, please, Sir."

When they arrived home, William helped Sarah off the buggy. He gathered her things with the toy train he bought and went inside. Later that evening, William told Sarah he had a surprise to show her. She went to the bedroom where William was sitting. "Come, sit beside me. I have something to show you. Do you remember when we first met? The train ride to North Carolina?" asked William. Sarah looked at him and said, "Yes. How can I ever forget? It was the best ride I have ever had. Why are you talking about it now?" William pulled the box from under the chair and said, "Look what I bought from the general store! When I saw it, I had to have it! It's a toy train set with the tracks and extra cars to go with it. It reminded me of when I first saw you. I have always wanted a train set. The first one I saw was in the Army. I wanted to buy one then, but I couldn't afford it. The clerk said I could pay for it in a few months. How do you like it?"

Sarah smiled and said, "It's beautiful! I saw you looking around the store, but I thought you were looking for tools. We need to keep this in a special place. For many years to come, this train will remind us of how blessed we are to have each other."

CHAPTER 10

•••

Spring was approaching. Sarah and William were getting to know their neighbors and church members. "I can't wait until Wednesday night Bible class. I saw Mr. Dockery on the job site today. He asked me if we were coming to Bible study on Wednesday. I told him we were coming, and he wants to know if I would teach the class this Wednesday. I am willing to do anything for the church. He also said that most of the members have a problem reading the Bible. You know Sarah, many years ago, when I was a boy, my grandma told us stories about her cousin named Harriet. She said that Harriet helped many slaves escape from their slave masters. She was a smart little woman. She also taught many slaves to read and make a mark for their names. I think that is where I get my spirit to help others," said William.

Sarah felt inspired. She looked at William and asked, "Is she still living? Harriet, your grandma's cousin?" William looked down at his folded hands and said, "Yes, she is still living. There was a home for the elderly in New York that she helped established. She took care of her parents for a few years, then after their death, she became disabled, and the family members had to admit her in the home. Some of these stories will never be forgotten. These are memories for a lifetime."

It was Wednesday evening, and William and Sarah loaded the wagon to go to Bible Study. Pentecostal Church of Christ was just about two miles away. It was in a small country town called Clemmons, North Carolina. There were only a few Negroes in this close-knit family neighborhood. Everyone knew and took care of each other. If you needed help with working in your fields, the neighbors would get together and help with the harvest. If the women needed help with their children, the mothers would come together and take care of children. Anything that a neighbor could do for you was done with love.

The church was full. Brother Dockery presided. "Let us all come together in prayer, brothers and sisters," he said. *"Our Heavenly Father, we come this evening thanking You for all your many blessings you have bestowed unto us. You said in Your Word, Lord, if any of you lacks wisdom, let him ask of God, that giveth to all men liberally, and up-*

braideth not; and it shall be given him. We all are lacking in many ways, Lord. Some need wisdom and some need understanding. Help us, Lord, to understand that if we are lacking in knowledge, you will give it to us. Never let us be ashamed to ask for what we need. It is you O' God who giveth the sun to shine, the rain, the wind and the moon by night. We are depending on you for all our needs. In Jesus' name we pray. Amen."

Brother Dockery introduced William. "Everyone who needs help with the Word of God, please raise your hands," said William. "I am going to help each one of you to read and understand what you are reading. God's Word should be plain for all to understand. I will be in prayer for you and your families. Let us get into groups. Maybe we can get a better understanding of what is about to happen. Turn your Bibles to the Book of Ecclesiastes."

William wrote a capital letter E on a chalk board and continued, "Look in the table of contents and you will find these words, 'Books of the Bible.' There will be two 'C's' after the 'E.' That word is ECCLESIASTES. Dose everyone have it?" he asked. All the husbands and their wives did as William asked.

"Now, I am going to read a few scriptures from this book. Listen very carefully. It is plain and you can understand what it means. Look at the passing of time—Winter, Spring, Summer and Fall. These are our seasons. We all know what our seasons are. God made this scripture plain to understand. One day follows another. Year after year. A decade. A century. It's swiftly passing. Time carries everything along with its sweep. Whence the value of time is great. God is eternal and above time. Men live in time and must consider it in all things. Men must learn that for everything there is a season, time and purpose. This is the third chapter of this book. I want you all to practice reading this scripture. It is easy to read. The main word is time. Everyone, repeat after me…time!" said William.

Brother Dockery thanked William for the fine job he did with his teaching. He asked everyone to continue to read the scriptures every night until the next Wednesday evening. Another brother in the church read the 27th Psalm and explained as the members listened. At 8 p.m., everyone sang a hymn together and the watch word was repeated.

When William and Sarah got home, she put the leftovers away. William gathered wood for the heater. When they were all tucked in for the night, they said their prayers and discussed the meeting before going to sleep. "I think we are going to enjoy our new church members. It's just a few of us. I think I need to see who needs more help with reading and allow them to try reading aloud. What do you think about that?" William asked. Sarah pulled the covers close to her face and said, "I think that would be a good thing to do. Good night, William."

The couple got up early for work as usual. Sarah continued working at the café and William worked at the college site. It was colder than usual. March was coming in like a lion. The farmers had predicted snow. They could tell by the circles around the moon and the squirrels gathering more acorns for the nest.

William was prepared for the worst. Sarah made sure he had warm underclothes and a heavy coat and hat for bad weather. At the end of the day, Sarah waited for William to bring the wagon closer to the entrance door. Mrs. Griffin watched as Sarah waited, and asked, "Do you have on enough clothes for this weather, Sarah? That small thin coat isn't warm enough for that wind out there. Come in here for a minute. I have a long heavier coat that you can have."

Sarah turned and watched Mrs. Griffin come from her room with a beautiful black wool coat. Mrs. Griffin held it up to Sarah to see if it would fit. "Oh yes! It looks like it was made for you. You can have it!" said Mrs. Griffin. Sarah thanked her and walked out the door to meet her husband.

It snowed all day that Thursday. It was cold and the snow came down like rain, but Sarah and William didn't miss a day of work.

The weekend was much warmer. They both worked on Saturday. They made enough money to pay their bills and had some leftover to save.

CHAPTER 11

•••

It was now May and William wanted to plant a small garden in the backyard. He asked one of the brothers at church to break the ground for planting seeds. Brother Mayfield came to the house that next Saturday morning. He had his mule and plow ready for work. The soil was rich and easy to break. He made two rows for each vegetable. In all, William had ten rows for planting seeds in his garden.

After a long week of work, William and Sarah bought seeds at the General Store. They purchased tomato seeds, cabbage plants, okra seeds, butter beans, squash seeds, and potato plants. Sarah had enough jars for canning the vegetables. They watched the weather to see when would be a good time to plant. "We need to get the seeds in the ground by next Saturday evening. The clouds look heavy in the west and that's a good sign of rain in a few days," said William.

Late Saturday evening, William and Sarah worked in the field until sundown. They planted all the seeds and plants. The next day, the rain came down—just a sprinkle to get the ground wet.

After Sunday morning service, they walked to the backyard. The ground was good and moist. "If it doesn't rain too hard this month, we will have a nice little crop. I just hope the birds and crows don't eat them before we do," said William.

Sarah prepared dinner and packed the lunch for the next day. Afterward, she walked outside and sat on the porch. William came out and they both sat quietly at home and enjoyed each other's company.

Sarah started work earlier the next morning. The menu was pig's tripe with onions, potatoes, mixed vegetables, collard greens, cornbread, and rice pudding. Miss Sue was there to help prepare the meals. After breakfast, while Miss Sue cleaned the dining room, Sarah started the dinner menu.

The café was so busy doing dinner, Mrs. Griffin decided to hire more help. She asked Sarah did she know someone who would like to help in the kitchen. Sarah couldn't think of anyone at that moment but told Mrs. Griffin that she would think about asking someone at her church.

During dinner, the café was packed. Everyone commented on the good meal Sarah prepared. Mr. Griffin told Sarah that any leftovers could be taken home for herself and William. She had plenty for William when he showed up at the back door that day.

After a few weeks, the garden began flourishing. The plants were about 12 inches high. William watched for birds and other wild animals. He made a scarecrow out of some old ragged clothes. Sarah made a wind chime out of some old tin pans. "I think that will scare the animals away for a while. This is our first garden and I want to reap from my first harvest," said William.

On Wednesday evening, the church members were at Bible Study, and everyone was in their proper places. Sarah greeted the women and the mothers of the church. "I would like to make an announcement before service," Sarah said. "My boss needs more help in the kitchen. Is there someone here who needs more hours to work? The pay is good, and Mrs. Griffin is a nice lady to work for. The hours are 5 a.m. until 5 p.m.," she continued.

One of the ladies who was sitting at the back raised her hand and said, "I would love to work those hours. My boss had to let me go from my other job. I know how to cook and clean. When should I go and meet her?" she asked Sarah. "What is your name, so I can tell her tomorrow about you?" The young woman got up to tell Sarah her name. She leaned over and whispered in Sarah's ear,

"Sister Brown. Thank you so much. God is a good God. When I got fired from my other job, I prayed to God to lead me to another one. He's always on time. I won't make you look bad. I will be on time and do my best."

William presided over Bible Study on this evening. Brother Dockery told him to take the floor and let God use him. "Everyone, turn to Ecclesiastes third chapter. Did you all get a chance to read over the verses from our last meeting?" William asked the members. One brother raised his hand to say he did. Another brother raised his hand, and his wife did too. Everyone in Bible class repeated the verse after William. Then William asked each person the stand and read alone. "That was good reading. I can tell that everyone practiced reading this week. If God allows us to come back next week, we will complete this lesson and go into some old-fashioned Bible study. We are going to take one book at a time. It can be from the Old or New Testament Let us all prepare to leave God's house," said William. When Bible study was over, Brother Dockery said the prayer and parting word.

Thursday morning was as usual. Another workday for Sarah was going to be challenging. The new waitress, Sister Brown, was going to start working in the kitchen. Mrs. Griffin greeted Sister Brown and explained to her the rules for working in the café. "I'm so glad that you decided to come work for me. My business has increased tremendously since I hired Sarah. She is my lead cook.

Just do what she tells you to do, and I think everything will be fine. She's all yours, Sarah!" said Mrs. Griffin.

Sarah wrote the menu on the board: Fried tripe, meat pudding, stewed dumplings, pork sides, cornbread, green beans and iced tea. The women worked together to prepare the meals for dinner. "Let us clean the tables and put away the breakfast plates. All the tablecloths have to be changed for dinner," said Sarah.

At noon, every table in the café was full. People came from the east, the north and the southside of Forsyth County. The Griffins name was singing all over the county. They didn't know who the cooks were, but the only thing they knew for sure was, those women could cook up a storm.

Mrs. Griffin was well pleased with the new girl Sarah recommended. She thought about giving Sarah a raise. She was the head cook in the café and she deserved more money.

On Friday morning, Sarah was the first person to enter the café. Mrs. Griffin met her at the back door. "Sarah, I want to talk with you before the other girls come in. My husband and I are well pleased with your work. We decided that you should get a little more money since you are the lead cook. We're going to raise your pay to $1 a day. I know it's not much, but it will help you and your husband get ahead on your bills. Marriage can put a strain on a new couple. When I first got married, we didn't have nothing but an old mule and one room on the back of his momma and daddy's house. So, this Saturday, you will get your raise," said Mrs. Griffin. Sarah thanked Mrs. Griffin for the extra money. She raised her hands up to God Almighty. "When the praises go up, the blessings come down. I thank you Lord for everything."

On Sunday morning, William and Sarah mounted the wagon and headed to church. There were more people this Sunday than ever before. The pastor was at the door greeting all the new families. As they were ushered in the church, one of the older members led an old spiritual hymn. Everyone joined in. William and a few of the other brothers stood near the pulpit. "Brother William will you please lead us in prayer and read a scripture of your choosing?" asked the pastor. William said an uplifting prayer and read one of his favorite verses. "I have shewed you all things, how that so laboring ye ought to support the weak, and to remember the words of the Lord Jesus, how he said, it is more blessed to give than to receive. I have read 35th verse of the Book of Acts, chapter 20. May the Lord add a blessing to the hearers and the reader of His holy word," said William.

After the sermon, the pastor asked William to do a review of the sermon and give the parting word.

"Lord Nelson, The Great English Naval Commander attributed his success to being 15 minutes ahead of Adolf Hitler, who left Munich, Germany on time before the bomb trains started. If you ride you must be on time. In religion, time is more important than any affair of life. And yet, so many of us are habitually late and the worshippers attention drawn away. To give reverence to God, demands all worshippers at their places, on time and take a part in the worship and service. You all have done a deed by being here on time. Now, may God watch and rule over us until me meet again. Let everybody say, Amen," said William.

CHAPTER 12

•••

It was Sunday afternoon and William and Sarah were sitting on their front porch, watching their neighbors walk up and the down the road. "You know, Honey. I'm thinking about buying another house. It's time for us to think about raising a family, now. This house is too small to raise children in. I rode over to a little town not far from here. Clemmons, North Carolina. It's just a few miles from here. Would you like to go see it? We don't have anything else to do," he said to Sarah. She smiled, eager to go.

It didn't take long to get there. They rode down a few streets and saw a house for sale sign on Lucy Lane. The house cost $800. There were three bedrooms, a dining room, kitchen, sitting room, front and back porch with an outhouse in the back yard. Two acres of land and $50 down and $8 a month. "This is a good deal for us. We have saved enough money to pay the down payment. My job is going to give me another raise. My boss told me that he appreciates me teaching some of the hired help to read. It really has made a difference on the job. With you working for the Griffins and making more money, I think we can afford this house," said William. Sarah didn't say a word. She was fascinated about the house and land. She has always dreamed of owning her own home. "If you like it, Sarah, I will talk to the owner tomorrow. Let's go home and pray about it. We need an answer from God," he said as he helped Sarah on the wagon.

•••

In 1907, Sarah and William bought their first home and moved to Clemmons, North Carolina. Mrs. Griffin, Miss Nelson, Miss Sue and Sister Brown, all helped Sarah decorate. They made curtains for the living room and kitchen. Some of the sisters from the church washed windows and mopped the floors. All the brothers from church got together with their wagons and helped with moving the furniture. Just one Saturday evening and everything was in place. Sarah was excited about her new home. She and William stood in front of their home and looked at what God had provided for them. "God has truly blessed us this year. We are going to serve Him more by being a service to others," he told Sarah as he stood in the yard thanking God for his blessings.

Sarah continued to work for the Griffins and William was working for the county. They were faithful in the church every Wednesday evening and Sunday morning. The pastor asked William to teach a reading class for the community. People came for miles just to learn more about the Word of God. William donated paper and wooden pencils for each person. One of the local general stores gave paper and books for the beginner readers. Clemmons township was prospering more that year than any other time in months. Every Sunday, the church members took up an extra offering for the learning class. Some Sundays, William would collect more than $2. He always prayed for the offering and for the giver.

Three Months Later

Sarah didn't feel well this cold winter morning. She turned over in the bed about 2 a.m. "What's wrong, Honey? You have been tossing and turning for the last hour," William asked while Sarah was getting out of bed. "I don't feel well. I need to go to the outhouse." She put on her coat and shoes and went to the back porch. She couldn't make it to the steps. She was sick to her stomach. In a few moments, she returned to bed. "Are you okay, Sarah?" William asked. Sarah held her stomach and said,

"I think I need to stay home today. I don't want to give the girls and Mrs. Griffin what I have. Would you please stop by the café and let her know?"

William arrived at the café at 5 a.m. Miss Sue was getting everything ready for breakfast. William knocked on the back door. When Miss Sue opened the door, she asked him, where was Sarah. He explained to her that Sarah didn't feel well. She didn't want to get sick on the job and make everyone else sick. She thanked him for letting them know, and to tell her they hoped she got better.

The next day, Sarah got up early and stood in the kitchen doorway. "William, I have something to tell you!" she said. William walked to the kitchen and looked at Sarah and asked, "What is it, Honey?" Sarah put her hands on her stomach and said, "We are going to have a baby!" William's mouth flew open! He didn't know what to say. "Are you sure, Honey?" he asked. Sarah told him, she was sure. William was so excited! He hugged Sarah and asked if she was okay, and did she need to stay home another day. She explained to him that she felt fine and needed to go back to work. He helped her on the wagon, and they went to work as usual.

Sarah helped prepare breakfast and wrote the dinner menu on the board. She looked around to see if everyone was busy. "Girls, I have some good news this morning!" Miss Sue and Sister Brown stopped what they were doing and gave Sarah their attention. "What is the good news this time, Sarah? You and William bought a new mule and wagon?" Sarah shook her head, looked at the women and said, "William and I are going to have a baby!" Miss Sue was speechless. She put her hand over her mouth and tears ran down her face. "Oh my God. A baby! I am so glad for you and William." Sister Brown threw her hands in the air and cried, "Thank You, Lord. They are having a baby, and I hope it's a girl!" The women were so happy for Sarah. They didn't let her lift anything over 10 pounds and told her to sit down, get some rest and don't get exhausted. Sarah refused to let them fuss over her. She told them that she would be fine, and she continued to work as hard as the other workers.

Nine Months Later

William and Sarah went to the general store for baby items. There was a handmade crib in the back of the store. Sarah walked to where the crib stood. She touched the wooden side and noticed that it had legs and it would rock. She motioned for William to come see it. "This is a good crib for this price. Do you want it, Sarah?" he asked. Sarah nodded. The manager of the store sold it to them for $1. "It's a little dusty, but it will serve the purpose. One of my neighbors made it out of some of his oak wood last winter. I told him it wouldn't be here long. Somebody is always having a young'un in these parts!"

Later that evening, Sarah stood in the bedroom. She felt a tightness in her stomach. She walked to the kitchen and called for William. He was outside gathering wood for the heater. "William, I think it's time. You need to go get the doctor." William stood straight up and ran to Sarah. "Are you sure, Honey? It will take me an hour to go and come back. Can you wait that long?" Sarah smiled and said, "I'm sure! I'll get everything ready for the doctor while you are gone."

William and Dr. Tillman arrived at 8 p.m. sharp! Sarah was in the bed. Her contractions were ten minutes apart. "Heat some water on the stove for me, William! Get it as hot as you can. Do you have the baby's clothes in reach?" he asked. William ran to the other bedroom and brought the new clothes Sarah had for the baby. "You can go in the other room, now. I will call for you later, Papa!" William smiled at Dr. Tillman and walked outside to the outhouse.

About 30 minutes later, Dr. Tillman walked to the next room. He called for William to come see his wife and new baby. "You got a fine baby girl in there. 8 pounds, 3 ounces. She is a big one! Beautiful as can be! Your wife is fine. Keep her warm for a few days, give her plenty of liquids and she will be okay," said the doctor.

William knelt beside the bed. He couldn't believe his eyes. His baby girl was as beautiful as her mother. "Honey, how are you feeling? Do you need anything? What do you want me to do?" William was so excited. He didn't know how to act with a newborn baby in the house. The thought of being a father for the first time in his life was overwhelming. Sarah opened her eyes and smiled. She looked at William and said, "Hey, Papa! You are a daddy, now! This is your little girl, Vivian. Her name means, 'lively one.' She will live a long life. Her memories will last from generation to generation. She will be strong and full of wisdom, even in her old age. I prayed to God for this child." As Sarah spoke, William noticed that she was going back to sleep. He pulled the covers over her shoulders and kissed her forehead.

•••

Everyone wanted to see the new baby. The church members bought food and desserts for William and Sarah. Mr. and Mrs. Griffin came later with a buggy full of baby clothes and toys. Sarah was so surprised and thankful for all her blessings. The pastor came after church on Sunday. "When are you proud parents going to baptize this beautiful baby?" I want to get my hands on her and bless this child. You must do it soon. I suggest about another week from now if that's okay with you!" said the pastor. William agreed.

The weather was getting warmer. Sarah was working at the café. Miss Nelson volunteered to keep the baby.

William became lead man on his job. He was making more money on the job and still had time to work in the community. Families from all over the region were moving to Winston-Salem. The big city was popular for its new tobacco company, "The Little Red Factory." There were Help Wanted signs all over town. William decided to stay at the school site and raise his family with help of the Lord.

Every evening at 5 p.m., Sarah, her husband and baby would travel the same two miles home. The baby was well taken care of, and everything seemed to be going okay.

The following week, William hitched the mule to his wagon. The mule acted like he didn't want to move. William got off the wagon and examined the animal. "What's wrong, William?" Sarah asked. William looked in the mule's mouth and saw that something was wrong. "I think our mule is sick. I'm going to ask Dr. Tillman if he knows anything about animal diseases," said William. He didn't want Sarah to worry about things that he could control, but in his mind, they were headed for trouble. It was going to be difficult to go to and from their jobs. Sarah saw the look of worry in her husband's eyes and said a silent prayer.

•••

William had to buy another mule and buggy. The

baby was getting older, and they had to have more room to travel from work, to church and for others who didn't have a ride. Sarah was working more hours and was now supervising the entire café. Mrs. Griffin retired because of a sudden illness. "We are going to make it, ladies. I really miss Mrs. Griffin and her good advice about the menu, but we are going to trust God and do our best," said Sarah.

Restaurants were on every corner now in Winston-Salem. People were migrating from Virginia, Raleigh, Greensboro, High Point, and other surrounding cities. The school was going to change from "The Slater Normal School" to "Winston-Salem Teacher's College." William had worked so faithfully for many years. He wanted to attend the college for a better education. But his family came first, and he had a daughter who would grow up and maybe, the Lord would bless her or her children to attend someday.

CHAPTER 13

•••

Twenty Years Later

What do people really get for all their hard work? I have seen the burden God has placed on us all. Yet God has made everything beautiful for its own time. He has planted eternity in the human heart, but even so, people cannot see the whole scope of God's work from beginning to end. So, I concluded there is nothing better than to be happy and enjoy ourselves for as long as we can. And people should eat and drink and enjoy the fruits of their labor, for these are gifts from God. And I know that whatever God does is final. Nothing can be added to it or taken from it. God's purpose is that people should fear him. What is happening now has happened before, and what will happen in the future has happened before, because God makes *the same things happen over and over again." (Ecclesiastes 3:9-15)*

William and Sarah had seven children now. William prayed to God every night to let him live to see them become adults. God has granted him his prayer. As he and Sarah rested on their front porch, he turned to her and said, "I want to meet with all my children. They are all grown now, and they must leave this nest to make families of their own. I want them to work as hard as we did. Get educated at the school where my hands help laid the stones. Have a family and educate them. And if God's plan for them to not marry, then love and help others the way we did. Don't have a 'counterfeit faith.' Evil people and impostors will flourish. The Word corrects us when we are wrong and teaches us to do what is right. God uses it to prepare and equip his people to do every good work. Patiently correct, rebuke, and encourage God's people with good teaching. I must tell my children about the passing of time. Keep the memories in the hearts and the children's hearts and their children's hearts and so on and so on," said William.

April 1932

Vivian decided to move to the big city of Winston-Salem, North Carolina. After the death of her parents, she needed to be more independent and get a better job. She was working at the café for the Griffins, but business was in the negative, due to fast growth and high demands from the public. One of her best friends, Reymona, traveled with her.

As they entered the bus terminal, there were three young men sitting in the café. "Girl don't look! They are watching you with all four of their eyes!" Vivian didn't look back. Reymona held her arm so tight, that she left her little fingerprint in her flesh. "What do you mean don't look back? If they are watching me, they got to be watching you too, because we are together," said Vivian as they walked pass the "White's Only" sign to the bathroom. When the girls used the restroom in the back of the café, they noticed that the men were gone. "Where did they go?" asked Vivian. The girls looked at each other and laughed because of their silliness. "Well, they don't know us, and we sure don't know them. Let's try to find a room down the street," said Reymona.

The girls walked for many blocks down Main Street. "Look, there's a sign on the window across the street. It looks fairly clean! Let's see if Coloreds can stay there!" said Vivian. The girls rang the doorbell. A tall White man came to the door. "Can I help you girls?" he asked. Reymona spoke up and said, "Yes. Don't you have a room for two vacant tonight?" The man asked them to come inside the building. He told them he had a room for two people, and it would be $2 per night. "We'll take it!" yelled Reymona. The girls examined the room and decided that it would be okay for a few weeks.

The next morning Vivian and Reymona got up early. They put on their best dresses and waved their hair to the side. Vivian wanted to wear her high heels, but Reymona suggested that they dress alike. She preferred her low heels for comfort. "I tell you what! You wear what you feel comfortable in and I will wear my high heel shoes. I feel comfortable in anything I wear." So, Reymona gave in. She wore her high heel shoes also.

The girls went from store to store, looking for work. No one was hiring. They decided to go across the street to sit in the park. The four guys that they saw at the bus terminal were sitting on a bench. One of the men spoke to Vivian. "Hello. Didn't we see you girls at the bus terminal last night?" Vivian looked at Reymona and said, "Yes. I remember seeing you, but we were trying to find a place to stay." The tall gentleman walked over to Vivian and asked, "Where are you staying? Wait a minute! I shouldn't ask a young lady a personal question like that. I'm sorry. I didn't introduce myself. My name is John Andy Evans. But you can call me Andy. And who do I have the pleasure of meeting?" Vivian offered her hand to the man and said, "My name is Vivian Clingman."

Andy moved to Winston-Salem to get a better job. He wanted to work, and some day have a family. He and Vivian continue to date each other for several months.

Meanwhile, Vivian got a job at the county school as a cook. She was a good cook; a trade that her mother taught her. She worked in the school cafeteria and made a decent salary. Reymona attended the community college and earned a degree in business.

During the latter part of 1932, Andy and Vivian decided to get married. "The first time I saw you, I knew you were going to be my wife. I love you with all my heart. I will do everything in my power to make you happy, Vivian. I'm not promising you that life will be easy, because it won't. I trust God first, and we will live each day to make each other happy. Will you please be my wife, from this day forward?" he asked.

In 1933, their first child was born, John Andy Evans. And two years later, their second son was born, James Henry Evans. Last, but not least, their third son, Robert Nelson Evans, was born. Vivian loved her boys. She worked hard to give them the best of whatever they needed.

•••

It was now December of 1938. Her baby boy was five years old. Vivian went to her closet and pulled out a long box. She asked the boys to come inside. "I have something to give you boys. My daddy bought this many years ago. He gave it to me and said it was to stay in the family as long as possible," she said. She opened the box and showed them the train set that her father bought for her mother. "My dad told me the story about this train set. I want you boys to have it. Always keep it in this box and place all the parts the way you found them. We are going to put it together every Christmas Day." The boys were excited about the train. They had never seen a train set like that one before. It was large enough to run in two rooms of the house.

So, every Christmas for many years, someone always remembered to get the train and set it up.

One Year Later

Vivian wanted to try one more time for a little girl, but nature wouldn't allow it. *"What's for me is for me. God will provide. Maybe, if it is God's will, one of the boys will give me a few granddaughters. It's all in God's hands,"* she thought.

CHAPTER 14

•••

The boys grew tall and handsome. John enlisted into the military. He found the love of his life while serving his country. He decided to get married and have a family. Vivian was so proud of him. He traveled all over the world and raised two beautiful girls. John would come home as often as time permitted. Coming to see their grandma and granddaddy was always exciting for the girls.

Soon, James was enlisted into the Army. He didn't want to go, but Vivian explained to him what being a soldier was all about. She asked him to come sit by her side and she said, "A soldier is many things, my son.

S is for Steady and Strong

O is for Optimistic and Outstanding

L is for Loyal and keeping a Level Head

D is for Diligent and Disciplined

I is for Intelligent, Immovable

E is for Earnest, Effective and Efficient

R is for Rational, Resourceful

Yes, a soldier is many things, but most of all, a soldier is someone's son. I love you! You boys are our heroes!" After serving, James decided to pursue an education. He had attended the school his grandfather helped build, Winston-Salem State University. He worked hard and studied harder to complete his four years and received his degree with honors.

His mother would tell stories about how her parents worked hard in that community. Winston-Salem would always be home, but just a few miles south wouldn't be bad, he thought. He applied for a teaching position he read about in the local newspaper. He went in the house and discussed the job with his mother.

"Mom, I found a job teaching school in Anson County. I think I will apply for it. Two hundred miles isn't too far from here. What do you think about it?" His mother took him by the hand and said, "No matter where you go, God will be there. You pray about this job and wait on God to give you the answer. I asked God a long time ago to stay with my children. He has answered my prayers. Don't ever do anything until you ask your Heavenly Father. He is the one who will guide your footsteps to the end of time. Apply for the job! If you get it, it was God.

If you don't get it, it was God." She patted the back of his hand and gave him her blessings.

James applied for the job. He was notified by mail to come to Wadesboro, North Carolina for an interview with the school's superintendent. He was so excited. "Mom, I got my answer in the mail! I'm to be in Anson County next Monday, at 10 a.m." His mother sat calmly, rocking in her chair, and said, "I knew it! When I saw you coming, I said to myself, 'That boy got that job!' Now, you get your new suit out and wear it. Shine your shoes and go get your hair cut. You want to look like somebody when you walk between those two doors. The way a man wears his suits says a lot about him. You boys are good looking if I have to say so myself. Yes Lord! You got that job!"

It was 1960. James traveled for three hours south to Anson County. He arrived at 8 a.m. The superintendent was a tall White gentleman who looked to be intelligent and very astute. James knew not to sit down until he was asked. The man offered James his hand and said, "Hello young man. I am the Superintendent of Anson County Schools. You can call me Mr. Wildermuth! Have a seat! I would like for you to complete a few important papers and then we will go into the next room across the hall to meet our Board of Education Members." James shook the man's hand and sat down to complete his paperwork.

Mr. Wildermuth introduced James. "Ladies and gentlemen, I would like to introduce you to James H. Evans.

James, you have before you Mr. Glenn Martin, Mrs. James R. Clark, Mrs. Fred Mills, Mr. Charles Ratliff, Mr. James A. Hardison, Mr. Arthur C. Summers, and Mr. W.E Steagall. This group of people here works together to provide the best education and facilities available for the young people of Anson County. Welcome Aboard!" he said.

The next week, James was introduced to several outstanding educators in the community: Mrs. D.D. Hammond, Mr. John Marable, Mr. Fred Worthy, Mrs. V.R. Covington, Mr. H.L. Price, Mr. L.H. McRae, Miss Aggie Hailey, Miss A. Armstrong, Mrs. C.C. Hooper, Mrs. M.F. Lindsey, Mrs. E.G. Horne, Mrs. A.P Waddell, Mr. Sherod, Miss Katherine Torrence, Mrs. A. S. Patton, and Mr. & Mrs. Frank Richardson.

James heard about a lady who owned a beauty salon in town. He needed somewhere to stay, so he decided to visit the large family home on Salisbury Street. This community was mostly Negroes. The streets were like Las Vegas. There were many bars, night clubs, restaurants, doctor offices, public library, barber shops, laundromats, clothes cleaners, convenient stores, car garages and a school for all the Negro children. He was excited to ride down the popular streets of Wadesboro.

The lady who had the room for rent owned a beauty salon next door to her house. This family was one of the most prominent families in the community. They enjoyed people and people loved to support her business.

She heard that a new teacher from Winston-Salem was coming to teach in the Lilesville community. Everyone was looking forward to meeting him.

James rode down the street and then came back up to take a second look. "I think this is the house. I need to turn around and drive in the yard," he thought. There were several cars in the driveway. A beautiful lady was standing on their front porch. She was watching as James drove in the yard. She motioned for him to stop on the side of her lot. "Get out and come in." She yelled.

James got out of his car and walked to the steps. "We are so glad to meet you." She said, as she reached for his hand. "My name is Freddie! This is my home. I have one son and a host of nieces and nephews. My brother and his wife live next door. I heard that you need a place to stay. I'm so glad you stopped here first. There are several places to rent in this neighborhood, but you must be careful where you lay your head around these parts. I have lived here all my life. I know most of these people in this neighborhood. If you decide to rent from me, I will introduce you to some of the elect in town," she said, as she walked through the house to show James the room.

It was a small room, but James was fine with that. He didn't want a large space, just large enough for his bed, dresser, television and his desk. "This is the room. If you need linen for the bed, there's a closet in the hallway with towels and sheets. The washer is on the back porch.

My rent is $20 a month. It's due on the 25th day of each month, no exceptions! Do you want it or not?" she asked. James looked through the room and looked out the window. He opened the closet and walked down the hallway to the bathroom, and said, "I'll take it! When can I move in?"

The next day, James moved in. He called his mother and told her about the people he was living with. She warned him about staying out late at night. She told him to always use his home training, because it represented the way he was raised. He told her he would be respectful, and he loved her very much.

Monday morning was the first day of school. James was in his classroom bright and early. He wrote his name on the left side of the blackboard and the date on the right. He cleaned each desk and placed a pencil and a sheet of paper for each student. He had a handout for his students that read:

Classroom Rules
1. Show respect.
2. No talking while the teacher is talking.
3. No chewing gum in class.
4. No fighting.
5. No cursing.
6. No smoking in the bathrooms.
7. No sleeping in class.
8. No eating in class.
9. No cheating on school assignments.
10. No running in class or hallway.
11. Come five days a week, ready and willing to learn.

CHAPTER 15

•••

James stood at the door as the students entered. As each student came through the door, he said, "Good morning!" When the bell rang, he closed the door and asked everyone to stand and give him their name. He noticed that he had more boy students than girls. He walked down the aisles between each row of desk and said, "My name is Mr. James Evans. I am from the big city of Winston-Salem. I have served my country and I have earned my degree to teach each one of you. We are here to learn about each other. The way I conduct myself will demonstrate what kind of person I am and the way you act will demonstrate to me the person you are. I hope we will be on our best behavior. Does anyone have any questions for me?" he asked.

Everyone sat quietly in their desks. James asked the

students to write their first and last names on the paper. When they finished, he collected the papers and recorded them in his class record book. He separated the boy names on one side of his book and the girl names on the other side. It was time for Bible devotion and the Pledge of Allegiance. He looked at his class roster for a student's name to read the devotion. When he looked up, he saw one of the boys talking without permission, and he yelled, "Earnest! Stand up and come forward. Take this Bible and turn it to the Book of Psalms chapter 23. Read it all, please!" The student got up and walked to the front of the class. As he opened the Bible, one of the boys in the back of class put his hands over his mouth and giggled out loud. James heard the young man and asked him to come forward. "What is your name, young man, and why are you laughing?" He didn't say anything. He was embarrassed to stand before the class. "Do I have to repeat myself?" James asked the boy. "My name is Johnny!" the boy said. "Well Johnny, you will lead us in the Pledge of Allegiance when Earnest is finished reading?"

Earnest opened the Bible to the 23 Psalm and tried to read without stuttering. James didn't know that he had a problem with reading aloud, so he told him to take his time and read it correctly. When Earnest took his seat, Johnny asked everyone to stand and say the Pledge Allegiance to the flag.

The boys could tell that James would be a teacher who

they could get away with anything. When the bell rang to change classes, they talked about their new teacher. "Did you see that man's shiny shoes?" one boy said. "And that suit is sharp as a tack! I think he is going to be the best teacher we have ever had. He's going to let us do anything we want to. I can't wait to go outside to the basketball court!" the boys said to each other.

At lunch time, everyone was talking about the new teacher, Mr. Evans! The girls got in a group and discussed the car he was driving. "I heard he was from Winston-Salem! How far is it from here?" one of the girls asked. They wanted to know if he was married and had children. One of the girls said she heard he was living in Wadesboro with a family on Salisbury Street. James was the subject for the rest of that day.

At recess time, James didn't tell the boys that he played basketball in college. He wanted them to think he was soft and didn't know every much about school or life. "Boys, you have to change into your P.E. shorts if you want to play. Go inside and I'm going to play with you." They all went inside the building and changed into their shorts and tee shirts. James went in the bathroom with them. He thought he smelled cigarette smoke. "Are you boys smoking in here? You know the rules, no smoking in the building! I have told you in the beginning, now I think I need to show you. Let's go back to the classroom. I need you, Earnest, Johnny, Crawford, and Willie. The others can wait on us outside. Take the ball with you," said James.

He escorted the boys back to the classroom. He opened his desk drawer and took out a wooden paddle with a handle on it. There was something engraved on the paddle. It was the words, 'The Golden Rule,' in large letters. He asked each one of the boys to turn around and touch their toes. When they did, he gave them a sample of the Golden Rule. One lick was all it took to get his message across. The boys were surprised and didn't tell the others what had happened, until they left the campus. James didn't have to worry about them smoking on campus anymore. They were the most respectful young men in class. They didn't talk out in class nor did they make fun of the other students. They had gotten a taste of Mr. James Evans' Golden Rule.

Some of the students lived in the rural area in the community. Their parents had to work the cotton fields during the late summer and fall seasons. Many students were absent from school for months. The boys were failing the classes. James visited the parent's homes and decided to offer his help. The students who couldn't afford to buy lunch were given free lunch in the cafeteria. He asked the cook to keep a record of the students who needed lunch. At the end of the month, the bill was paid in full by James Evans.

He loved the students and wanted the best for each

one. If they needed clothes, shoes, or coats for the winter, James would make a house visit and made sure the need was met. The parents thought of him as a friend and mentor for the neighborhood. The school board was pleased to hear of all the good things he was doing in the community of Lilesville.

Years had passed. Most of the students he taught his first year had graduated from high school. Some of the boys joined the military. Some went away to college. Others got married and made their home in other parts of the state. James was a good teacher and they appreciated everything he did for them. They never forgot about his "Golden Rule."

CHAPTER 16

•••

During one School Board meeting, the board decided to move James to another position. They offered him a job as principal of another school in the county, East Polkton Elementary School. He was thrilled to get that promotion. That weekend, he went to visit his parents. He couldn't wait to tell them the good news. "Son, I told you to put your trust in the Lord. He will not lead you wrong. How're they treating you down there? You look kind of thin around your waist. Do I need to cook something for you to take back with you? I want you to get enough to eat!" said Vivian.

James told his parents he was doing okay, and yes, he got enough to eat at work. "I like where I stay, mom. The family treats me like I'm part of their family. I met a nice young lady at school. Her name is Elsie White.

She is a secretary in the office. She is a member of the Church of Christ in Anson County. I'm thinking about asking her out for dinner. I sure hope she says, yes! I get lonely at times when I'm not working," said James.

"Well, if she doesn't go out with you, let me know and I will write her a letter about my son. A woman would be crazy not to go out with my sons. You hold your head up. Keep trusting God and always do the right thing, and I guarantee it; that woman will go out with you and will make one of the best friends you ever had. Trust God on that!" said Vivian.

James was loading his car to go back to Wadesboro. His mother came out behind him and said, "Son, I have something special for you. I bought it on sale at the new department store downtown. I wanted you to have this. Don't ever loan it to anyone. It's for you, and you only!" James looked at his mother and asked, "What is it, Mom?" She handed James a big brown box. He thanked his mother and kissed her.

He carried the box to the porch and opened it carefully with his pocket knife. He opened the box. It was a large Oxford Brown Samsonite suitcase! It was large enough to carry all his clothes, shoes, important papers for school and his caps. "Mom, this is the best thing you could have bought me. Now, I can go and come in style. This will last me a lifetime." He loaded up the car to leave. As he was going out the door, he turned and

hugged his parents and said, "I love you so much, Mom. You have always been a good mother to us. I pray for you every night. If life permits, I will be here for you and Dad, with the help of my Savior, Lord Jesus Christ."

As he drove to Highway 109 South, tears flowed down his face. His mind went back to how his parents encouraged him to go to school and make something out of himself. "I have submitted my plans to you God. You are in control and has better plans that will come to pass, in your perfect time," he prayed.

As he drove down Salisbury Street, he wondered about the people who needed so much help in the community. One of the Baptist churches was across the street from his home. He wanted to visit the church and get to know their members. He saw a car parked at the rear of the parking lot. "I don't know whose car this is, but maybe they can give me some information about this community," he thought, as he entered the church lot.

When he got out of his car, a tall man opened the side door. "Hello, young man. I'm Pastor Williams. Who are you?" James shook the pastor's hand and introduced himself.

"I saw your car, and just wanted to come over to greet you. I'm James Evans. I live with the Lewises across the street. I work at one of the schools in this county. My home is in Winston-Salem and I attend church there, also," he told the pastor. The pastor was happy that James thought of the church and its members. He invited James to attend anytime he wanted to. He also discussed the neighborhood, and mentioned that poverty was on the rise because of poor management or the lack of income.

James drove across the street to his home. He took his new suitcase out of the car and carried it inside the house. When he got to his room, he unpacked his clothes and opened the suitcase. In his room, there was an envelope with all his accomplishments and awards in it. He examined each one and put them in his new suitcase. He thought about where he should keep it. It was too large for his closet, so he decided to keep it under his bed, saying to himself, "Yes, this will work!"

Monday Morning

James was given the directions to East Polkton School. It was only about seven miles from where he lived. He got there at 6:30 a.m. The custodian was there to open the doors and start the heat system. When James got out of his car, a thin tall Black man greeted him at the entrance door and said, "Come on in. We are so glad to have you at our school. I'm the janitor here, just call me Dan."

James walked in. Dan directed him to his office and gave him a tour of the school. "The teachers will be here around 7 a.m. and the buses will arrive between 7 a.m. and 7:30 a.m. We have a lot of children here. This community is small when it comes to us. Most of the people who live in Polkton are White. Good land here! I made my home down the street from here. Yes, Lord! Polkton has been my home for many years. My momma and daddy raised 10 children and we all picked cotton, cropped tobacco and picked peaches for a living. But you know what! God took care of us! He made a way for my momma and daddy to educate all 10 children. All of us didn't go to college, but we finished high school. Let me shut my mouth so you can start your work," he said, as he walked away with his broom in his hand.

It was almost 7 a.m. James decided to go to the entrance door and greet each teacher. Everyone was on time and waiting for their students to exit the buses. He greeted each student with a "Good morning!" and they excitedly greeted him back. When everyone was in their proper places, James made an announcement on the intercom and said, "I would like for all students and staff to meet in the auditorium at 9 a.m. Please exit your rooms in an orderly manner."

The auditorium was filled with teachers and students. James stood at the podium and made his announcements. "My name is James Evans, your new principal. Greetings to you all. I would like for all my teachers to stand, starting with the first graders." The teachers stood and gave their names and asked all their classes to stand, also. James discussed the requirements for each student and teacher while they were on the campus. "This is going to be a great year for East Polkton School. We must work together to reach perfection. You all may leave now, starting with the first graders. Have a great day!" said James.

After lunch, James visited all the classrooms. He wanted to greet each teacher personally. They were excited to have him as their principal. One of the teachers raised her hand to get his attention and asked, "I would like to ask if we may plan a welcome event for you, Mr. Evans? It would be nice to involve the students and have them to make their own welcome notes." James said it would be nice for the children, but as for him, he felt welcome when he drove in the parking lot.

The teachers worked hard on their special project. Each student made their own unique card or letter. The teachers got together and made a huge banner to hang in the auditorium. The janitor, the cooks and even some of the parents were included in the celebration.

One of the teachers went to the office to make the announcement. "May I have your attention? May I have your attention, please? Will all the teacher and students please come to the Auditorium, starting with the first graders?"

James was sitting at his desk. He heard all the commotion. "Well, I guess they forgot to include their principal. I haven't heard them call for me yet." About 10 minutes later, a little girl knocked on his door. He asked her to come in. She had a sheet of paper in her hand and read, "Welcome to our school Mr. Evans! On behalf of our teachers, students, and all our staff members we welcome you. Would you please follow me to the Auditorium?"

James was so surprised. He thanked the little girl and asked, "What is your name?" She smiled and replied, "My name is Betsy!"

James and Betsy walked to the auditorium. Everyone was there. The teachers decorated the auditorium from front to back. They had flowers and banners. The children made cards and wrote letters expressing their gratitude. James was asked to come to the podium, so the students could read their greeting cards. The cafeteria workers and parents prepared food and brought covered dishes from home. There was plenty of food for everyone!

After everyone was served and seated, the high school band came from the back entrance of the school and entered the Auditorium. The children were so excited to have the band there. They stood up clapping, yelling, and dancing to the beat. East Polkton School was on fire with excitement!

For many years, James enjoyed his stay in Polkton. He found a church that was affiliated with his church from home. He was invited to come for a visit by one of the staff members.

If there was a need in Polkton, James was there to help. He knew that when working in the county, there was always something to give—either yourself or your donations. It was time to give of himself. He knew there would be another promotion, but he didn't know when or where.

CHAPTER 17

•••

A few years later, James was contacted by the superintendent to come to his office. "Oh my! What is it now?" he thought to himself. "I'm getting older now! I must take better care of myself. Whatever they need me to do, I will prepare myself for the job."

The school board asked James to be the assistant to one of the principals in the county, Dr. Truman at Wadesboro Central School. James was pleased to assist. He thought about his parents and decided to go home to share the good news.

James traveled to Winston-Salem the following weekend. When he arrived, there was bad news about his father. He had taken ill a few weeks earlier, but his mother didn't want to worry him. She knew if she had called, James would have been on his way home. "James, your father is sick and had to be hospitalized. You know we are getting older and can't stay here forever. We belong to God. When He gets ready for us, we must go. I gave you boys, my husband and myself back to God a long time ago. We must be obedient to His will. So, when you go see your father, let him know that it's okay to go be with the Lord. Think about how I raised you all. Trust God and he won't fail you," said Vivian.

One week later, James' father passed away peacefully. For many weeks after the death of his father, the ride to Winston-Salem would never be the same. He now had his mother to think about. She was all alone in that big house. He decided to go home every weekend. The job he had now was less stressful.

The new job at Wadesboro Central School would be a challenge for James. The need to ensure the safety of children was a task he was familiar with, but now this leadership position included interactions with the teachers, other administrators, board members and parents. He knew some of his days would be unpredictable. Behavior problems were on the rise and he was not a disciplinarian. James preferred instructional leadership. Before demonstrating his 'Golden Rule' he would give the students instructions on how they should behave. He loved enforcing the attendance rule. He knew the importance of coming to school every day. Sitting down with the students alone gave him a chance to explain the importance of a good education. He would call the student's parents and ask if he could come to their homes to discuss a student's behavior or learning problem.

Each day after work, James would go home and pray for the students and their parents. Reading the Bible gave him that zeal he needed to go the extra mile. As he sat in his bedroom, one of his father's sayings came to his mind, "No matter how successful someone may become, when God is not in their life's equation, things simply don't make sense." James put his Bible away. "I will go to work with a new outlook on life and leave the other business to God," he said before going to bed.

•••

The position at Central School lasted for many years.

James was getting near retirement age. One day, while reading the local newspaper, he saw a picture of a young woman who was assigned to be principal at a new school in the county. Wadesboro Primary School was going to open soon. The new principal was the little girl from East Polkton School. "I cannot believe my eyes! This is the little girl who made me a beautiful card when I first came to this community. She is all grown up, finished college and now working in the school system. It doesn't seem real. Time has passed me by," James said, as he read the paper again to make sure he was reading correctly.

The next day, James received a letter in the mail. It was from the Central Office. The school board offered him a position as Assistant Principal at Wadesboro Primary School. He smiled and said to himself, "They want me, as old as I am! My time is almost over. Those students will run all over me, now." The idea of James working at his age was unheard of. His footsteps were getting shorter. He had a crack in his voice and his hair was gray. "How would the children react to an old man like me?" he wondered. But he remembered that he was taking his supplements and drinking his nutrients every day. "I'm going to accept the position and stop working when God tells me to stop," he thought.

James called the superintendent and thanked them for the job. The superintendent told him that he was highly recommended for the position.

His mother was up in age, nearly 100 years old now. He would take some of the nutrients with him for his mom. He believed that the vitamins he was giving her would help her live to see 100. It wasn't guaranteed, but what was it going to hurt?

As he traveled the 109 North Highway, he would catch himself daydreaming about his past. He thought about his father and how hard he worked for his family. Now that his mom was of age, he wanted to do all he could for her. "I would love to get someone to come in and help around the house or pay some of the church members to come in for a few hours. I'll ask someone before I leave this weekend," he thought.

James looked at the sign on the side of the road. He had been so lost in thought, that he didn't realize he was already in Winston-Salem.

He got out of the car and looked to see if his mom was at the door. When he walked to the front porch, the door was locked. He unlocked the door with his key and went inside. He saw his mom in a wheelchair. He dropped his suitcase and ran over to her and asked, "Mom what happened! Why are you in this wheelchair?" She looked at James and smiled. "Don't you worry none, boy. I have a hard time getting around in this house, so my doctor ordered me this chair. I'm glad he did. I can go anywhere in this house," she said. James was relieved to hear that. He hugged his mom and sat down on the sofa.

She asked him about his job, and he told her about the new position. "I told you boys to trust God in everything you do. He won't lead you wrong," said his mother. James' mom told him that she wanted him to take some of his things with him. "Your train set is still in your room. I want you to take it with you. It's gathering dust under that bed. You can enjoy it with the children in your school. Let them see it when you have a special activity day at school," she said.

James thought that was a great idea. The train set was in the same box that it was bought in. He pulled the box from under the bed and cleaned it off. He took it outside and put it in the trunk of his car.

The next day, James went to church and took his mom with him. After service, he asked some of the women if they knew of someone who would stay with his mom for a few hours a day during the week.

One of the women told him about a lady who was looking for a part-time job. She gave James the woman's name and phone number. He thanked her and they left to go eat at their favorite café.

When they returned home, James called the woman for more information. The woman told James she would love to stay with his mother. He asked the woman if she was from Winston-Salem area. She told him that she was actually from Wadesboro, North Carolina. James was surprised to know that. "Could you tell me more about yourself? I live in Wadesboro, too! I'm the assistant principal at one of the schools there," said James. The woman asked James for the address to his mother's house and told him she was coming over to see who she was talking with and to meet his mom.

Shortly thereafter, a tall Black woman got out of the car that pulled into the driveway. She walked to the porch and knocked on the door. James came to the door and greeted her. "Hello, I know you! Mr. Evans is your name! I remember you from school" the woman said. James was shocked! "Yes. Yes. Who are you related to in Wadesboro?" he asked the woman as he offered her a seat. "I live on Coley Hill. My mom and dad had 10 children. I'm the third child. I moved up here about thirty years ago and now I'm retired. The lady who you talked to at church is one of my friends. I need something to do during the week. I have two girls who are grown and living on their own," she said.

James was glad to hear that the woman didn't have another job. Maybe this would work out fine. He was thinking about asking her to stay more than a few hours a day. The two made an agreement. The woman was to come in the mornings to prepare breakfast and stay until noon to prepare lunch. Light house duty was added to the agreement. James felt good about having someone from the town he was working in to come and stay with his mom.

When he returned to Wadesboro, he wanted to see where the Coley Hill community was. To his surprise, it was just across the street from where he was living. "I have passed this street many times and didn't know it was called Coley Hill!" he thought, as he walked through the neighborhood.

He saw a big brick house on a hill and decided to walk to the door. As he got closer, a woman came to the door and asked, who was he looking for. James greeted the woman and said he was looking for Coley Hill. The lady smiled and said, "This is it, what's left of the hill." She asked him to come in, and the conversation started.

"My husband and I have five girls and five boys. One of my girls lives in Winston-Salem. I heard you are from that area, also" said the woman. James nodded as she spoke. He told the woman that he was a principal at the new school in Wadesboro and he thought he knew most of the people in the community. "What church does your family attend?" he asked the lady. She told him that she and her family attended the Methodist Church on Salisbury Street. "That is where I live. Do you know a lady named Freddie?" The woman told him yes, Freddie was her hairdresser. "Did you say you work at the new school? I have a daughter who works there, too. Her name is Irene. She works with the special needs children. You might know her!"

James said he didn't know her but would go in the E.C. Department at work and ask for someone with that name. "The reason why I walked over here, I met one of your daughters in Winston-Salem. She will be working for my mother part-time. Your home is nice and inviting. I see you have your Bible on the table. It's good to meet nice people and I have met a lot of nice people in this community," said James.

James left Coley Hill and went to his home. He took the suitcase and the train set out the car.

CHAPTER 18

...

The next week was going to be busy. Evaluations were scheduled and learning materials were ordered to determine areas of improvement. James always did his best and tried to be fair when it came to the teachers. He didn't know all of them, but he would observe them in the classroom with their students. If there was a need for improvement, he would be the first person to offer his advice. No job was too hard for him.

The buses were another problem. Parents complained about the bus drivers and the drivers complained about the students. It was something new every day, but James prayed about all the problems and God made away for him to move forward.

...

Saturday morning went as usual. James began packing his suitcase for the trip to Winston-Salem. The report he got from the sitter was good. His mom was getting more attention from the doctors and home health caregivers, so James decided to take her to church this Sunday. When he arrived at the house, Vivian was sitting on the porch. She was in a happy mood. "Hey son," she waved. He was so glad to see that she was doing well.

He got out of the car and grabbed his suitcase. "Hey Momma. You look good this morning. I'm so happy that you are outside enjoying this beautiful weather," he said. She smiled and held his hands in hers. "I can always depend on you, James. Are they feeding you, boy? You look thin around your waist," she said. James smiled but didn't respond. He knew it was her mind.

He took his bags inside and looked around to see if everything was in place. The house was clean, and his mother had everything she needed for the next week. He went back outside and asked his mom about going to church on Sunday. He knew she would enjoy seeing some of her old friends and church members. "Mom, we are going for a ride!" he told her, while helping her to the car. She looked at James and asked, "Where are you taking me, boy?" James smiled at her and said, "We are going to Lewisville! I just thought about my grandma and granddaddy. It's good to look back at our past. I miss the countryside and the buildings. We haven't been to Lewisville in years. So, today, let's enjoy the ride and enjoy each other." He helped his mom into the car. He had a pillow for to sit on. He wanted her to be able to see without straining her eyes.

No matter what street he turned on, his mom knew the people who lived there and knew if they were living or dead. When they turned onto Lucy Lane, she got excited and yelled, "That's the place where we lived when I was a child. Lucy Lane was the first street my parents lived on. My momma worked at that café for many years. And look James, that's the house my momma lived in when she got off the train from Virginia!" Her eyes lit up like a Christmas tree. James answered her every time she told him to look. He knew that going back to her old home place would get her sweet spirit up. They rode to the Little Red Factory. The old memories were good for his mother. He hadn't seen her that happy and smiling in a long time.

He decided to go to the old café for lunch. When he turned the car into the parking lot, she looked at the sign and asked, "Are we going to eat here?" James smiled and said, "Yes, Momma. I want to taste some of their good ol' home cooking." He helped his mom in the wheelchair. A young man came to the entrance door and assisted the two in the café. Everything was different from years ago. "My God in heaven, boy! This place is beautiful. Look at all these nice dishes and glasses. And the floor has carpet from the front to the back of the dining room. I wonder who the owners are now?" she asked. Before she could finish speaking, a tall young girl came to their table and said, "Welcome to Griffins Café! May I get you something to drink?" The waitress laid two menus on the table for James. He gave one to his mom and asked her what she wanted to drink. She told James, all she wanted was a sweet glass of tea and make sure it was sweet! James ordered her a sweet tea and water for himself. His mom could not get over how nice the café was. She talked about her first time coming there. She knew all about the old building and how it looked years ago.

Soon the waitress brought out their meals. His mother had fried chicken, collard greens, fat back, cornbread and mashed potatoes. James had the same. When they had finished their meals, the waitress laid the ticket on the table and said, "Don't rush yourself, I'll come back and get this later."

Vivian leaned over and asked, "What did she say?" James said, "She said she will come back and get the money for the food we ate." Vivian wanted to know how much did the food cost, and said, "I hope it's not a lot. I could have cooked this myself!" James didn't say anything. He got his wallet out to pay for the meals. As he laid his wallet on the table, he saw the waitress coming towards them, pushing an old woman in a wheelchair. It was Mrs. Griffin! She was still living and looking well.

The young woman rolled the chair next to Vivian. It was a surprise! James told his mom to turn around and look. When she did, tears of joy rolled down her cheeks. The two old ladies looked at each other and reached out to hug. "I can't believe it's you Vivian," the woman cried.

It had been years since James' mother had heard anyone call Mrs. Griffin's name. "My God in Heaven! I thought you had passed away," said James' mom. Mrs. Griffin looked at Vivian and said, "Oh, no! You are thinking about my mother. I'm her daughter. My mother didn't have any children when your mom worked for her. I was born a year after you. We are a year apart in age. My mom died when I was 20 years old. They left everything to me, including the café!" James was relieved for his mother's sake. He was thankful that the woman got it straight. He didn't want his mom going back to Winston-Salem, spreading that news on the phone. They all thanked each other and said their goodbyes. James loaded his mother's wheelchair in the car and headed back home. The conversation about the Griffins continued until they drove in the yard.

When he opened the door to push his mom inside, the phone was ringing. It was the sitter! "Just calling to see if you and your mom are okay!" The following week was going to be busy for Vivian. Doctor appointments, an eye appointment and going to the podiatrist was scheduled for the same week. "Yes, we are fine. Make sure

Mom wears a sweater when you take her out!" James told the sitter. She was all he had left. He loved her and wanted to do all he could to make sure she was well taken care of.

The next day, the sitter called and gave the good report from all the doctors. "Your mom will live to see 100, if she keeps this up!" said the sitter. The sitter was surprised to hear how Vivian explained to the doctors about her medicines and how often she took them. She knew everyone at the doctor's office. She could remember when her next appointment was and what time to come. "My mom is a smart woman. She's been like that all our lives. When my brothers call, she can tell the day and time they called!" James smiled, as he was talking to the sitter.

CHAPTER 19

•••

Assessing data for the state standard tests was a job James enjoyed doing. It was going to be stressful this year because there were more children at Wadesboro Primary School than the other schools he served. His main concern was the children. He knew that the best preparation for them was to make the best scores by building skills and master reading and math. Then they would perform better on their tests.

James loved to challenge the parents when it came to the children in his school. He would always stress to the parents that they were their children's first teacher. The parents loved and respected James. During the Monday evening parent meeting, questions were asked about ways parents could help their children at home. James had an answer for all the parents—less play, more reading and starting with the Word of God! After the meeting, James met with some of the parents in the hallway. One parent wanted to thank James personally for what he did for her child, and added, "If it wasn't for you Mr. Evans, I don't know what I would have done this winter. I didn't have money to buy shoes for my children, and you went out of your way to bring me the money. I want you to know how much I love you, and God loves you more." James' heart was full. He was thankful that God had made a way for him to help someone else who really needed it.

Throughout his entire teaching career, James didn't only help the children and parents in the school system, he helped the people in the community, also.

•••

Another school year had passed by. James was cleaning his office for the summer. He wanted to stay with his mother for a month or two, but there was so much work to do in the community. He always attended Vacation Bible School at the local churches in town. The school board decided to have a short session of summer school for the third graders. James couldn't give up the chance of working with the students.

So, he went to Winston-Salem every weekend as usual. He got up early the next Saturday morning and put all his important papers in his brown suitcase. Before loading the car, he went back inside to check for everything. There was an envelope under his pillow. "What is this?" he wondered. It was $500 in cash that he forgot to give the children who made improvements on their tests. Each child was to get $50. He got in his car and headed to the school. The principal was in her office. He knocked on her door and said, "Hi. You know, I forgot to give the students their reward for testing! I need to send their money to them." The principal assured him that she would ask the secretary to mail each student a check. James was relieved. He didn't want to disappoint his students.

James arrived in Winston-Salem at 4 p.m. He unpacked his car and carried everything into the house. When he looked around for his mother, he didn't see her. He went into her bedroom and there she was, in bed and asleep. He watched her for a moment and then touched her foot and whispered, "Momma, Momma are you awake?" She didn't say anything at first, then she slowly opened her eyes. "James, is that you?" she asked softly. James sensed something was wrong. He wanted to call the doctor and then he thought about calling the EMS. "Momma are you sick?" he asked. She turned on her side and said, "Yes!"

Vivian dreamed great dreams for her sons, and then she allowed them to chase the dreams they had for themselves, and she loved them just the same. James' heart was broken because the time had come. He thought about some of the things his grandfather would say about "time." A time to cry and a time to laugh. His time to cry had come.

His first love was transitioning to the great beyond and he would never see her again in her flesh. A time to be born and a time to die was a season for promotion. His mother had lived over 100 years and he was thankful. God was preparing his mother all those years for this promotion. But still, he felt selfish about her leaving so suddenly.

James stood over his mother's bed and stroked her hair. In his heart he spoke the words, "Mom, your hands were busy through the day. You didn't have much time to play the little games your boys asked you to. You didn't have much time. You had to wash our clothes, sew, and cook. And when we brought our picture books and asked you to please come share the fun, you would say in that soft voice of yours, 'A little later son.'"

July 2010

Arrangements were made for James' mother. There were many acts of kindness and prayers for the Evans family. That sweet, sweet spirit of Vivian Evans would never be forgotten.

CHAPTER 20

•••

The ride to Winston-Salem would never be the same. James' work was not finished. He wanted to retire from the school system, but he didn't want to leave the students and his friends. One day while sitting alone in his room, he noticed the obituaries of his parents. He looked at each picture and thought, "I need to know more about my past. Mom was a beautiful woman, but who is she and where did she come from?" He decided to research his family tree. He started with Vivian's family first. For months, he found out new things about himself and her family. "I have cousins right here in Winston-Salem!" he learned.

On his father's side of the family, it was difficult to find out what he wanted to know. That didn't stop him. He went to the county library and found information about the Evans tree. All the paperwork he gathered, he put in his suitcase—over 50 pages of research about his family and there was more to collect.

August 2010

Another year of schoolwork and students began. James was past the age of retirement, but he loved his job. The school board called a meeting and discussed James' position. He would remain the Assistant Principal and he would be the Bus Monitor.

For months he did his job well. Each day was a challenge. His body was weakening. A time for every activity under the heaven, had come.

In 2010, James retired from the Anson County School System. Fifty years of service was completed.

"What do people really get for all their hard work? I have seen the burden God has placed on us all. Yet God has made everything beautiful for its own time. He has planted eternity in the human heart, but even so, people cannot see the whole scope of God's work from beginning to end. So, I concluded there is nothing better than to be happy and enjoy ourselves as long as we can." (Ecclesiastes 3:9-12)

After retirement, James continued to work. He truly enjoyed the fruits of his labor. He knew it was his gift from the Almighty God. He gave to charities. His monetary gifts helped the children who attended school. He gave to the college foundations. He donated funds to local organizations. His work was never done.

People from all over the county knew Mr. Evans for his kind acts of love. Many took advantage of his kindness and gifts, but he prayed for them and asked God to forgive them. He knew he was doing the will of God!

One afternoon, James heard about a book written by one of the girls who lived on Coley Hill. He was interested in anyone who was doing positive things in the community. James asked the sitter to stay overtime that afternoon while he attended the book signing luncheon at the county library. The library and one of the book clubs in town sponsored the event.

When he arrived, there to his surprise, was a familiar face. The young woman who wrote the book turned out to be a friend of his. Irene Harrington had worked in the school system with him. James went in and got a seat close to the podium so he could hear her story. He was amazed at how well she spoke. Her book, "Coley Hill," was about family history. He understood where she got her title from. After lunch, he greeted the author and said, "Hey! You did a beautiful presentation of your book. I would like to buy 10 books—one for myself and I'm going to give the other ones to my friends and relatives." Years after the first book, Irene wrote four more books and James attended each book signing event.

The relationship he had with his friends grew closer. James didn't stop attending the churches, school activities, local meetings and going back to Winston-Salem to attend his own church.

CHAPTER 21

•••

Sickness struck again. James' landlord and friend, Freddie, was ill. James was the main overseer of the home. The time for a sitter had come. "I'm going to take care of her the way I cared for my mother," said James. The home health agency provided services for Freddie in the home. Friends and family members visited each week and offered whatever help was needed.

God's greatest gift to us is time. Freddie's time had come. All the pain of this world was over. James thought about the first time he met Freddie. She was a kind woman. She loved people and loved her family. "There are friends, there is family, and then there are friends that become family," he believed.

Life was different now for James. He continued to be a friend to all who needed help. The sitters for Freddie offered to do the house chores for him. He had someone to wash his clothes and prepare his breakfast. At lunch and dinner time, he would always go the neighborhood restaurant, The Hub. Home-cooked meals were served every day except Sundays and Mondays.

James was asked by the principal at the school to come by and visit the children. Whenever he walked the halls of the building, the students would gather around him to say hello. He could name each child and knew who their parents were. "Are you doing your best in school this year?" he would ask. The answer was always the same, "Yes. I made 100 on my test this week! Yes! My Math teacher said I did great on the quiz today!" James would leave an award for each student. The principal made sure of that!

•••

On Monday morning, James had scheduled a doctor's appointment. James' diabetes was under control. He had lost weight by walking up and down the stairs in the basement. He knew what to eat and he drank plenty of water during the day. The home aides who worked for him were encouraged to do the same. "Get on the scales, girls. Don't over eat! Go to bed early and get your rest! If you need some multi-vitamins, I can order you the best ones to take," he would say to the them every morning.

THE SUITCASE

James got up early on Saturday mornings to travel to Winston-Salem. He wanted to attend his church and see some of his old friends and relatives. After church, he got a phone call from one of the brothers from college. "Hello! I'm doing great, and yourself! Yes, I bought my black suit this time! I think I can make it!" he told his friend. WSSU Alumni was giving James a surprise retirement party. Everybody who was somebody would be there. "They should have given me more time to prepare for this! I could've asked my friend, Miss White to come," he said, as he unpacked his suitcase.

•••

The banquet hall was filled with guests and Alumni members. Everyone stood when James opened the door. An usher led him to the Guest of Honor's table. James looked around and saw Miss White standing near his seat. The Mayfield family, the Steeles, Brother Hamlin, the Browns and the Dockery family were there. James looked to his left and saw his principal and staff members. And, most importantly, his brother and his family were standing on his left side at the table. The food was catered by the Alumni Association. The tables were decorated for a king!

During dinner, each organization sponsor went to the podium to say something about James' accomplishments. When the event was over, each guest placed an envelope in a large bowl that was used for the centerpiece. Then one of the brothers presented the bowl of gifts to James and added, "Most things we do in life are habitual patterns we have been taught since childhood. James, you had good parents. They are smiling in glory tonight because their sons made them proud. You didn't have to do everything, but you picked your essentials in life and you stuck with them. My brother, may God continue to be a blessing in your life." Another brother stood and said, "A flood of favor is coming your way. You have done your best. Keep the faith and God will do the rest."

James stood to give honor to all who participated in the event. Tears streamed down his face, and he quoted an old hymn.

May the works that I've done speak for me.
When I'm resting in my grave, there is nothing to be said.
But may the works I've done speak for me.
May the life that I've lived speak for me.
When the best I've tried to live, my mistakes He will forgive.
Let the life that I've lived speak for me.
May the service I give speak for me.
When I've done the best I can and my friends don't understand;
May the service I give speak for me.
The work I've done seems so small.

Sometimes it seemed like, I've done nothing at all.
But when I stand before my God, I want to hear Him say,
'Well Done.'
May the works I've done, speak for me.

There wasn't a dry eye in the building. People were embracing each other and trying to get to James for a hug.

As he rode back home, he couldn't help but think about his parents and his brothers. "Lord, you truly blessed my family. If I don't ever find another family member in this world, I thank you for the family that I have. We are small in numbers and blessed with Your love," he prayed.

When James arrived, he took his things inside. He opened his suitcase and poured the envelopes inside. He wanted to relax and take time to read each card. He saw the family Bible on the table. Reading the Word before bed was one of his favorite things to do. "Satisfy us each morning with your unfailing love, so we may sing for joy to the end of our lives. Give us gladness in proportion to our former misery! Replace the evil years with good. Let us, your servants, see you work again; let our children see your Glory. And may the Lord our God show us his approval and make our efforts successful. Yes, make our efforts successful. Amen, Lord!" he prayed.

James sat quietly in his lounging chair watching the

ball game. He pulled the suitcase close to his chair. When he opened it, he found a note that was placed in the bowl. It was from one of his neighbors from Wadesboro, and read, "I didn't have any money to put inside my letter, but I wanted to say, thank you for all you have done for me and my children. You blessed me in secret, and I pray that God blesses you openly. Don't ever think God doesn't know what you did. I pray that when your time comes, God will send someone to help you. This will be a person who you never expected. That will be your secret blessing. Again, thank you!"

CHAPTER 22

•••

One December morning in 2019, James picked up the newspaper and began to read. The World Health Organization had declared a public health emergency of international concern because of a mysterious disease outbreak in Wuhan, China. It was being called the COVID-19 pandemic, also known as the Coronavirus pandemic.

"Symptoms of COVID-19 are highly variable, ranging from none to life-threatening illness. The virus spreads mainly through the air when people are near each other. Recommended preventive measures include social distancing, wearing face masks in public, ventilating and air filtering, hand washing, covering one's mouth when sneezing or coughing, disinfecting surfaces, and monitoring and self-isolation for people exposed or symptomatic," read the article. "My God, what has happened in the world years ago is coming back to us in year 2020. God is going to shake this world like never before!" he thought as he read.

COVID-19 made headlines all over the media. People in China were shown on television wearing face masks and they were dying every hour of the day. Soon the spread of the disease hit the USA. America waited too late, thinking that this was only going to happen to foreign countries.

James' parents had told him about the Great Depression, and how it affected the world with many people dying from starvation. "My daddy told me about Black Tuesday! I will never forget how tears ran down his face. People suffered severely back then, and now it's coming back to this generation, but in another form. It's going to take a lot of us out. We just don't know what God is going to do this time. If you don't know the Lord, you better find Him and find Him quickly!" he told the assistants who helped around the house.

The first American case was reported on January 20, 2020. The president declared the United States outbreak a public emergency. Restrictions were placed on flights arriving from China. But the initial United States response to the pandemic was otherwise slow, in terms of preparing the healthcare system, stopping other travel, and testing. The President remained optimistic on the future of the coronavirus in the United States.

James would listen to the news every night. If there was something that he thought his friends and family members needed to know, he was the first one to notify them.

He bought cleaning supplies, masks, and disinfectants for his home and car. One day, while in the grocery store, he noticed that the food shelves were empty. He went to buy cases of water and the shelves were also empty. While walking through the store, he saw one of his friends buying groceries. "Hello, Mr. Evans!" his friend yelled. "Do you need help finding something?" he asked. James looked in his grocery cart and said, "Yes! I see that you need help too!" The man smiled and said, "You are right! All the milk and bread are gone. What in the world are we going to do?" James looked at his friend and said, "Do what we should do every day—pray and trust God!"

The two men chatted about the virus and how Americans were rich compared to other countries around the World. James and his friend knew the Lord! Whatever happened, God was still on His throne.

•••

By February 2020, new cases were being reported around the country nearly every day. Many were people who recently returned from China, including a student from Boston and a woman in California. Two more cases of person-to-person transmission were reported in California.

"Girls, I want you to wear your masks at all times. Do like they tell us to do—wash your hands before you do anything in this house. We must be obedient," James would warn.

He believed in doing what was right.

CHAPTER 23

•••

The whole world was paralyzed with fear. People would look at the news and hope that the virus would pass them by. State after state reported climbing death tolls. Hospitals were filled with sick and dying people. The virus was spreading fast.

"The United States has only a fraction of the medical supplies it needs to combat this virus. There's going to be a shortage of surgical masks and respirators too. They have waited too late," James would say to his friends and caregivers.

Beyond the gloomy outlook for the physical health of the nation, James was concerned about the welfare of the students. "We are going into 2021 soon. Modern technology was needed years ago for our schools. The poor families can't afford food. How in the world are they going to meet the needs of their children?" James wondered. He knew the rural places in the county. Some families didn't have Wi-Fi or Cable. "Anytime you need to use a computer for anything, you need Wi-Fi. I'm going to let the school and churches know, if they need assistance with computers in the home, give me a call. I will donate funds for some of the children," he would say. Everyone knew James was willing to help whenever and wherever there was a need.

By March, coronavirus cases reached 100. States including New Hampshire, Colorado, Nevada, Tennessee, New Jersey and Maryland announced their first cases. James read the reports in the newspaper. The virus was getting too close to home. His only nieces lived in the state of Virginia.

He would send up prayers daily for his family. He was a great uncle now and was proud of it. The thought of that baby getting the virus was frightening. *"My family is slowly fading away. God, please save my family members and others who have family members sick with this virus or in the hospitals. Save the land, Lord. You did it for my grandparents and I know you can do it again,"* he prayed.

James knew the word of God. "If my people who are called by my name will humble themselves, and pray and seek my face, and turn from their wicked ways, then I will hear from Heaven, and will forgive their sins and heal their land. That's in the Old Testament. People don't

believe the Bible is true, but it is. God performed miracles form the old prophets and He will perform miracles
today," he explained to his workers.

One of the girls who helped him was washing the
breakfast dishes. She turned around to face James and
said, "I don't read my Bible every day, but I do read it. I
want to be like you James. I want to be able to tell others
about God. I try to talk to my children about the Lord,
but they don't listen to me." James got up from his chair
and got his Bible and said, "You see this Book? It's nothing to play with. This is the Holy word of God himself. If
he says, 'study', that's what he means. When you study the
word, you must open the Bible. Don't leave it on the table
for decoration. Take God's Word serious."

James knew that there would come a time when the
Word of God would work for His people. If he could only
get them to read and understand "time." There's going to
be a time for everything under the sun.

•••

James called his nieces to ask if they were okay. He
worried about the virus coming their way. The COVID-19
pandemic-associated economic shutdown created a cri-
sis for all workers, but the impact was greater for wom-
en, non-white workers, lower-wage earners, and those
with less education. "This is pitiful!" thought James. "The

Black community will be affected the most by this virus. What will our people do without jobs?" James decided to change the television channel from news to sports. He had enough of the subject, COVID-19.

Still, he couldn't escape it. Several countries across Latin America imposed restrictions on their citizens to slow the spread of the virus. Restrictions were all over America including in the grocery stores, schools and even the churches. Restaurants were closing and businesses were gone.

Soup kitchens sponsored by the local churches in the community offered James the opportunity to sign up for the service. James was reluctant to do so. He had always been the one to give charity, not take from it. He thanked the committee and told them he would be fine.

James' sitters made sure he had everything needed for the home. Going to Winston-Salem every weekend was canceled, because churches were closed, and his friends didn't accept visitors. He would communicate by phone with the pastor and the message was recorded every Sunday and Wednesday evenings. One of his close friends would call and advise James to stay home and wear his mask. James would respond in a Christian manner. He thanked his friend and let him know that he always wore his mask and washed his hands.

CHAPTER 24

•••

One of James' friends who lived on Coley Hill was working for a homecare agency. It was late one Thursday evening in November when she received a phone call. "Hello, who is this?" she asked the person on the other line. "I have tried to call you all day. James is sick and I couldn't think of anyone else to go check on him!" the voice said. His friend was puzzled that the sitter would call her. She had never called her before and wondered why she was calling her when she should have called 911! The sitter continued her conversation and said, "I have the virus and I can't go up there. I don't think he has anything to eat. Could you go check on him for me?" she pleaded.

James had always been there for his friends. She didn't hesitate. Tired from working all day, she stopped what she was doing, and went to see her friend.

She lived only about seven miles from James' home. As she pulled in the driveway, she noticed his car was parked in the yard and not in the driveway. She got out of her car and walked to the side door. When she knocked on the door, she saw that the door was open. As she called James' name, she opened the door and walked in, and said, "Hello, Mr. Evans. How are you doing tonight?" In a soft calm voice he answered, "Okay!" His expression showed he did not recognize her. "Your sitter asked me to come check on you. Have you had anything to eat?" she asked. James answered her and said, "Yes!"

His friend noticed that his hands and voice were trembling. "Now, who are you?" he asked. She walked closer to him so he could hear her clearly. The two masks that she was wearing made it difficult for him to hear her. "This is Irene. I'm your friend from Coley Hill."

She began to looked in the refrigerator for food and water. There were only a few boxes of chicken dinners from a restaurant. It looked as if he was trying to eat, but perhaps his appetite was gone. She asked him if he wanted some water, but he refused.

Irene cleaned the areas in the house which he used the most—the kitchen, sitting room and the bathroom. James sat on a stool near the kitchen and watched as she went through the house.

She noticed that he acted as if he was cold. He had on

his bearcat school jacket and a black cap. "Are you cold, Mr. Evans?" Before he could answer, she felt his hands, and they were cold. She decided to check the thermostat on the wall. It was on cool. "I'm going to turn the heat up a little," she said.

James wanted to watch the ball game. Irene asked him if he was going to bed and he said, "No! I will go after the game." She told him that she would return the next day and bring him some lunch. The next day, around 10 a.m., she called James to see what he wanted to eat. "I like vegetables and bring me a sweet tea" he told his friend.

One of the local restaurants were serving dinners to go. She ordered him a plate with stewed chicken, steamed cabbage, and a baked sweet potato. When she arrived with the food, James looked at her and said, "I can't have the tea because it will run my sugar up." His friend didn't know that he was a diabetic. She poured him a glass of water and explained to him that he had to eat all of his food and drink plenty of water. James stared at her with tears in his eyes. He didn't move his fork. He never touched the glass of water. He sat on the stool and stared at her. "Look what you have—sweet potatoes, chicken and cabbage!" He didn't speak. She touched the back of his hand and pinched the skin to saw if he was dehydrated and he was! So, she decided to offer James the food by feeding him. He opened his mouth and began to chew. She noticed that while he was chewing, it appeared to her that he didn't swallow the food. Then she held the glass so he could swallow the food. "Mr. Evans, you take your time and eat what you want. If you don't eat it all, put the leftovers in the refrigerator. I will be back in the morning to finish washing your clothes," she said.

Irene got up early the next day and drove to James' house. She knocked on the door. The door was unlocked, so she walked in greeting him with a "Good morning!" James was walking through the kitchen with only a T-shirt and pants on. He looked confused and disoriented. "They want me to go to the hospital, but I'm not going anywhere!" he said, as he looked at his friend. She went to the dryer to get his clothes. "Have you had anything to eat this morning?" she asked. James walked back to his seat and said in a soft voice, "No."

She looked in the refrigerator and saw the leftovers from Friday afternoon. "What do you eat for breakfast, Mr. Evans?" He looked at her and said, "Two boiled egg whites and one slice of toast. That's all I want." Irene looked at his medicine organizer and saw that he had not taken his medicines for days. Then she asked, "Have you taken your medicine for today?" He answered, "No." She took the package for that date and gave him the pills. There were injections in the refrigerator, but James could not tell her his dosage.

When she looked around again, James had not eaten the eggs and took only a sip of water. She asked, "Who told you to go to the hospital?" He told her that the sitter came to see him last night and said he needed to go, but he told her he wasn't going anywhere. Irene said, "Mr. Evans, I think you should go!" He held his head down and said, "Okay, I'll go."

James went to his room to put on a shirt and get his coat and hat. He stayed longer than his friend expected. She decided to see what was taking him so long. When she looked in his room, he was sitting on the side of his bed, staring into the distance. He looked like he was day-dreaming, and he didn't have his shirt or jacket on. "Let me help you with your shirt. Which one do you want to wear?" she asked. He pointed to a long sleeve blue shirt. She put his arms in the shirt and helped him with his coat and hat. "Are you ready to go?" she asked.

James walked to the dining room area and asked, "Where is my money?" His friend was shocked because she didn't know he had money in the house. "Don't worry about your money. I will look for it when I come back," she said. "Here are my keys to the house and car. You keep my car keys!" said James. Irene took the keys and told him that she would take care of the house until he came back home. "Don't you worry about anything. Just go and let the doctors check you out," she said.

She assisted James to her car. She put his mask on his face for protection. As she drove to the hospital, a thought came to her mind, *"It doesn't look good, Lord.*

He's a diabetic. He hasn't taken his medicine in days. Not eating. Not drinking. I know he is dehydrated. I hope and pray that it is not that virus."

The hospital was about three miles from where James lived. They drove to the emergency entrance. A nurse came out with a wheelchair and said as she opened the back door to the car, "Hello! Is this Mr. Evans? Hello, Mr. Evans! Let me help you out!" James smiled at the young nurse and said, "Hello!"

Everyone at the hospital seemed to know who James Evans was. They made a chart for him and asked Irene, "Is it COVID-19?" She looked at the nurse and said she didn't know. The nurse wanted to know if she was related to James. She told them that he was a dear friend of hers. "Who should we put down as the next of Kin?" one of the nurses asked. Irene spoke up and said, "All of his relatives live out of town, but you can put my name and phone number down."

As they rolled James to the examining room, Irene said a silent prayer for him. "Lord, please don't let him have COVID-19. Take care of him like you have done for so many of your children!"

Early Sunday morning, Irene went to check on James. "I'm here to see James Evans. I brought him in yesterday!" she told the receptionist. The young lady looked at her and asked, "Are you the next of kin to Mr. Evans?" Irene explained to them that all his family members were out of town, and the Emergency Contact information was in his wallet. "If you tell James to send me his wallet, I can call his nieces who live in Virginia!" The nurse told her that they couldn't do that because of the HIPPA laws. "We are going to ask Mr. Evans to give us his relatives' names and we will look for the numbers. If he has them, we will call you. Give us your name and cell number. We will tell them to contact you, and they will give us permission to inform you about Mr. Evans," said the nurse.

James' nieces were informed that he was doing well and wanted to speak to him. "Uncle James, how are you? This is Joanna and Allison!" they said. James was surprised that they knew about his illness so quickly. "I'm doing better, now. I want you girls to call my friend, Irene. The nurse will give you her phone number. She has the keys to my house and car. Whenever they release me, she will be the one who will come get me. I love you girls so much. Don't worry about me. The Lord will take care of me. I must go now, talk to you later. Bye, bye!" he said.

James knew that his nieces would take care of all his personal business. He would brag to everyone how smart his nieces were. Although they lived in another state, that did not stop them from checking on their Uncle James. He was their only uncle on their father's side of the family.

After speaking with their Uncle James, the girls called Irene. They shared an instant spiritual connection. They chatted like they knew each other for years. "Uncle James told us that you took him to the hospital. We want to express our gratitude. Thank you so much for what you have done," they said.

The next day, Irene went to the hospital to talk with the nurses about James' progress. "Ma'am, are you relative to Mr. Evans?" She told them that she was not, but his nieces gave her permission to inquire about his condition. The nurse looked at her chart and said, "Oh yes! I see where his niece, Joanna, wants Irene to inquire about his condition. Are you Irene?"

The nurse walked with Irene to James' room. "Miss, you can't go in, but we will bring him to the window so he can see you." James was sitting on the side of the bed eating lunch. He looked up and saw Irene standing near the window. One of the nurses told him that his friend was waving her hand, so she asked him to wave back. He looked so happy and relaxed. The nurses told Irene that they remembered Mr. Evans from their Elementary School. "He was always so kind to all the students. He taught our parents. Someone told us that he worked in the school system for over 50 years. He had to be a real Christian to work with some of those kids!" they joked.

Irene wondered why were they taking all the extra precautions! She knew that everyone had to wear a mask and wash their hands because of COVID-19. No one ever said he had the virus. So, on her way out, she asked one of the nurses. "Does Mr. Evans have COVID-19?" He answered, "Yes! Ma'am, if you have had any close contact with anyone you think or suspect they have been exposed, you need to be tested. Call this number and ask for an appointment. They will give you the results."

Irene was tested for COVID-19. The results were negative. Eight days later she tested again. The results were still negative. Irene knew the power of prayer. She had a praying mother who knew that if you work the Word, the Word would work!

When she left the testing site, she didn't wait to go home and kneel at her bedside to pray. She prayed before the test and after she received her results, *"God, I thank You for what you have done in my life. What I did for my friend, Mr. Evans was from my heart. He needed help. I entered his home without knowing what I was about to face. I tried to protect myself by following the rules. There was no time to fear. Although others told me not to go, I went knowing that You and You alone would be with me. Now, Lord, I'm going to take this test. If there is anything inside of me that is not your will, take it out of me! From the top of my head to the bottom of my feet, I release it right now, in Jesus' name, Amen."*

The next day, a call came through from Virginia. The hospital was sending James to a rehabilitation center in Charlotte, North Carolina, where he would be for about six weeks. "Irene, could you please go to the house and pack Uncle James' suitcase and take it to the hospital? They are going to take him to Charlotte tomorrow. He wants his cell phone and charger. Thank You so much for what you do!" said his nieces.

His clothes were packed and taken to the hospital. James stayed in rehab for weeks. He called his friends and his church members. The brothers of the church would record the morning sermons and send them to him. Soon he was over the COVID-19 virus. However, in the weeks to come, his health declined and had to be transferred to the main hospital in Charlotte.

The news media were reporting more facts about the virus. "There is not enough data to show whether people with diabetes are more likely to get COVID-19 than the general population. The problem people with diabetes face, they are more likely to have worse complications if they get it, not greater chance of getting the virus. Also, the more health conditions someone has (for example, diabetes plus heart disease), adds to their risk of getting those serious complications from COVID-19. Older people are also at higher risk of complications if they get the virus."

•••

In December, Irene received another phone call from Virginia. James' health was declining for the worse. It was a matter of time.

"So, I saw that there is nothing better for people than to be happy in their work. That is why we are here! No one will bring us back from death to enjoy life after we die." (Ecclesiastes 3:22)

Three days after Christmas 2020, the news was all over the community. Mr. Evans had passed away. Some people believed it, and some could not grasp the bad news. People were calling Irene to see if it was true. Over and over again, the answer was the same, "Yes, he passed away early this morning!"

James knew that everything was meaningless on this earth. He asked the question so many times, *"What do people get for all their hard work under the sun? he understood that generations come, and generations go, but the earth never changes. The sun rises and the sun sets, then hurries around to rise again. The wind blows south, and then turns north. Around and around, it goes, blowing in circles. Rivers run into the sea, but the sea is never full. Then the water returns again to the rivers and flows out again to the sea. Everything is wearisome beyond description. No matter how much we see, we are never satisfied. No matter how much we hear, we are not content. History merely repeats itself. It has all been done before. Nothing under the sun is truly new. Sometimes people say, 'Here is something new!' But actually, it is old; nothing is ever truly new. We don't remember what happened in the past, and in future generations, no one will remember what we are doing now."* (Ecclesiastes 1:3-11)

James lived a Christian life. He worked faithfully in his church and neighborhoods. He wanted to please God and be a servant to man.

A time for embracing had come.

CHAPTER 25

...

James' nieces had to come to Winston-Salem to plan the Homegoing Celebration for their uncle. They had talked to Irene several times on the phone, but nothing was like seeing and embracing each other in person. "We are going to fly to Charlotte and rent a car to come to Wadesboro! Will you be able to meet us at the house in about an hour?" asked one of the girls. Irene agreed to meet them at the home.

The big house on Salisbury Street in Wadesboro, was no longer lively and inviting. The doors were locked so no one could enter. The windows looked dark like a moonless night in spring. The yard was full of pecans that the trees produced for their season. The old swing on the porch was silent because of the rust and decay in its joints. There was no more looking out the window to see the people come and go to the church across the street. The grass was tall as the weeds and wildflowers that grew in empty spaces on the lawn. This old house seemed lifeless now.

The girls pulled into the driveway around noon. Irene was sitting in her car, eagerly waiting to meet them. Joanna got out of the car first, followed by Allison. "Hello! I'm Joanna and this is my sister Allison. Sorry we can't hug and see what we look like, but we can elbow touch each other." Irene introduced herself and walked the girls inside the house. It was cold and the only sound they heard was ticking of a clock on the wall. They could smell someone's scent, but no one was there except the three women.

They walked to James' room and opened the door. "Oh, Uncle James!" one of the girls cried. They looked at the pictures on his wall. They touched his shirts and suits. "I remember this jacket. He wore it to my house one holiday!" one said.

As they looked around the room, they saw many quotes about the Lord, written on pieces of paper. "He was a spiritual man. He would tell us Bible verses without opening his Bible. I am so sorry that he had to leave us this way!" cried Allison.

The girls had to make the arrangements for their uncle. Because of his sudden death, they needed information for the Homegoing Service. "We don't have anything to start with making arrangements. I wonder, where did Uncle James keep all of his important papers?" they asked.

Joanna, Allison, and Irene looked all over the house for important papers concerning their uncle. Finally, they decided to look under the bed. "Old people would put their money, mail and anything else that they thought was important under their bed," said Irene.

The girls took the top mattress off and laid it against the wall. To their surprise, they hit the jackpot! Everything was under the bed. "Look at this! I remember this train set. My daddy has one, also. This thing is older than I am!" said Joanna, as she picked the big box up off the floor and dusted it off. She opened the box as the others watched. "Uncle James would bring his train set to my grandmother's house every Christmas, and our dad would bring his. They would put them together for us on Christmas morning. We've got to have this. I really think he saved it just for us," said Joanna.

They continued to look for all his accolades from schools, college and church. They searched the closets and the dresser drawers, but they didn't find anything important. The girls took a break to thank Irene for all she had done for James. Many questions were asked about the city and all of James' friends in the community. It was always the same good news about their uncle. "He was the last relative we have on my father's side. My grandmother only had three boys, and we are the only grandchildren in the family. They wanted to know how Irene and their uncle met and they were thankful that God sent her to help him.

"When we honestly ask ourselves which person in our lives means the most to us, we often find that it is those who, instead of giving advice, solutions, or cures, have chosen rather to share our pain and touched our wounds with a warm and tender hand. The friend who can be silent with us in a moment of despair or confusion, who can stay with us in an hour of grief and bereavement, who can tolerate not knowing, not curing, not healing and face with us the reality of our powerlessness, that is a friend who cares."

The girls continued to look around the house for more papers. "Let's lift this box spring up and see if there's anything else under here," said one of the girls. They all got a corner of the box spring and lifted it to the wall. "What is that?" asked Joanna. It was a big brown suitcase. It was so huge that the girls had trouble trying to pull it out. It was stuck behind the headboard of the bed. They grabbed and pulled until finally, they got a hold of it and pulled it out. "Oh, my God!" yelled Joanna. It was their Uncle James' suitcase that his mother had bought him when he finished high school. It was a little dusty, but in good condition. "I can't believe he kept this suitcase all these years! The outside is just the way it was when I saw it at my grandmother's house. He would bring it every time he visited Winston-Salem. Let's look inside!" said Allison.

The girls cleaned the suitcase off and opened it. "This is everything we need. Look how organized it is! I think he saved all these papers for us." said Joanna. Allison looked up at the ceiling and said, "Thank you, Uncle James!"

Now, the girls could make the arrangements for James. They packed everything in the trunk of their car. Allison told Irene to keep the keys to the car and house, until further notice. "The Homegoing Celebration will be Saturday, January 2, at noon. I will send you the address to the church," added Joanna, as she pulled out of the driveway and headed up the highway.

The next day, the girls called and said they had a safe trip back to Virginia. Everything was ready for service on that Saturday.

People would call from all areas in the community. They wanted to know when and where were they laying him to rest. Sympathy cards were mailed to the funeral parlor for the family.

Due to the restrictions from the Governor of North Carolina, the church could only have a limited capacity for the service due to COVID-19. The service reflected the way James lived his life—not too many people and not too many words spoken. Only close friends and family attended. James was a man who believed in keeping things decent and in order. He didn't want the family to shed tears of sorrow, but tears of joy. He had lived his life and accepted the call from his Maker.

Brother Brown stood and greeted the family and offered words of comfort. "For we know that when this earthy tent we live in is taken down (that is, when we die and leave this Earthly body), we will have a house in Heaven, an eternal body made for us by God himself and not by human hands. We grow weary in our present bodies, and we long to put on our Heavenly bodies like new clothing. For we will put on Heavenly bodies; we will not be spirits without bodies. While we live in these Earthly bodies, we groan and sigh, but it's not that we want to die and get rid of these bodies that clothe us. Rather, we want to put on our new bodies so that these dying bodies will be swallowed up by life. God himself has prepared us for this, and as a guarantee he has given us his Holy Spirit. So, we are always confident, even though, we know that as long as we live in these bodies, we are not at home with the Lord" (2 Corinthians 5:1-6). "*And just as each person is destined to die once and after that comes judgment, so also Christ died once for all time as a sacrifice to take away the sins of many people. He will come again, not to deal with our sins, but to bring salvation to all who are eagerly waiting for him*" (Hebrews 9:27).

"Church, Brother James has lived his life. The way he lived speaks for him. I don't have to stand here and give a long sermon about him, but there are three things I want to say, and I will be finished. We know that these old bodies are tents. We know these tents will dissolve. We know that God has provided a building for us, not made by man's hand," said Brother Brown.

The service was turned over to the funeral director. Everyone was dismissed except the family. As the girls exited the church to the cemetery, there was a soft spiritual voice in the midst, that seemed to say, "Farewell Uncle James. You have fought a good fight. Your spirit is with your grandmother Sarah, your grandfather William, your momma and daddy, your brother, and my dad. Go, and rest in peace."

"Nature gives to every time and season some beauties of its own; and from morning to night, as from the cradle to the grave, it is but a succession of changes so gentle and easy, that we can scarcely mark their progress."
                                                                    - Charles Dickens

CHAPTER 26

•••

Everything was getting back to normal. The news was still going around about Mr. Evans' death. "What are we going to do without Mr. Evans on Salisbury Street?" his friends asked, as they passed his home. Every week, Irene went to the house to start his car. When she opened the door, his scent was present. James' gloves, mail, ink pens, and even some of his clothes were still in his car. She saw one of his Bibles on the back seat. Curious, she opened the Bible and found a letter written in his handwriting. He had started a family tree for his family. The writing was so clear. She read aloud, "My grandparents were Sarah and William Clingman. Her mother was Harriet Tubman's cousin. My great-grandmother was a slave, but I don't know her name, nor her parent's names. Sarah was my mother's mother. My mother grew up in Forsyth County. She married Daddy there, too. We had smart parents. God blessed my ancestors. I don't know who I am, where my bloodline started, and where it will end. God will take care of me like he took care of my ancestors. Harriet Tubman's blood is in me. This woman was famous."

The paper was folded and placed in the Book of Ecclesiastes 3rd. chapter. On a separate sheet of paper was a paragraph that quoted, "God has ordained seasons in our lives. It's easy to get frustrated when our dreams aren't coming to pass on our timetable. When that happens, we have to submit our plans to God and trust that he is in control and has a better plan that will come to pass in His perfect time."

She put all the papers back in the Bible and left it on the back seat. *"Mr. Evans was a good man and he loved helping people. Maybe he wrote those letters hoping that the right person would find it. He never got married and didn't have children. It was all in God's plan,"* she thought.

James was a nice friend to Irene. They didn't visit each other like most of his friends did, but she believed that he knew in his heart, if he ever needed her to come, she would be there with no strings attached.

Our God works in mysterious ways! *"For His thoughts are not our thoughts, our ways are not His ways, declares the Lord. For as the heavens are higher than the Earth, so are His ways higher than our ways, and His thoughts than our thoughts."* (Isaiah 55:8-9)

CHAPTER 27

•••

A month later, James' nieces returned to North Carolina. They called Irene to ask if she could meet them at the house in the next hour. When they arrived, she was sitting in her car. They all got out of their cars and went inside the house. "We can't thank you enough for all your help! How is everything going with you and your family?" asked Joanna. Irene said that she was doing well.

"I have something to show you girls," said Irene. "I found this Bible in Mr. Evans' car. I think you need to read what he wrote on these papers," she told Allison and Joanna. The girls sat down on the sofa and opened the Bible. "Oh, my Lord! This is what he started doing months ago. He wanted to know more about his ancestors. He talked to me about doing research on the Evans and Clingmans, but I didn't know he started and found this information. These are memories that will last us for a lifetime. We never knew about our great-grand parents. My grandmother Vivian told us about when she lived in Lewisville, and a little about her childhood, and that's all we knew," said Joanna.

Allison and Joanna embraced each other. They looked at Irene and said, "We are going to break the rules today." The three women hugged, and tears of joy flowed down their cheeks. "You just don't know why God does the things He does. If it wasn't for Uncle James meeting you and your family on Coley Hill, I wonder, who would have come to help him? I believe that you were in God's plans years ago. Uncle James was to go when and where the Lord wanted him to. The COVID-19 didn't take him out; it was God our Lord and Savior."

•••

"So, the greatest test in life is to see whether we will hearken to and obey God's commands in the midst of our storms of life."

The tests of James' faith developed perseverance, which led to maturity in his walk with God. He knew what the Word said, that testing was a blessing because when the testing is over, and we have stood the test, we will receive the Crown of Life.

EVANS FAMILY PHOTOS

...

THE EVANS FAMILY
ANDY, VIVIAN, JOHN, JAMES & ROBERT

JOHN, JAMES & ROBERT EVANS

JAMES EVANS' FIRST SCHOOL

HENRY GROVE SCHOOL
LILESVILLE, NORTH CAROLINA

CPSIA information can be obtained
at www.ICGtesting.com
Printed in the USA
BVHW072331100921
616547BV00015B/755